The Wrong Brother

Also By Bree

Historical Romance:

<u>Love's Second Chance Series</u>
#1 Forgotten & Remembered - The Duke's Late Wife
#2 Cursed & Cherished - The Duke's Wilful Wife
#3 Despised & Desired - The Marquess' Passionate Wife
#4 Abandoned & Protected - The Marquis' Tenacious Wife
#5 Ruined & Redeemed – The Earl's Fallen Wife
#6 Betrayed & Blessed – The Viscount's Shrewd Wife
#7 Deceived & Honoured – The Baron's Vexing Wife
#8 Sacrificed & Reclaimed – The Soldier's Daring Widow
#9 Condemned & Admired – The Earl's Cunning Wife (soon)
#10 Trapped & Liberated – The Privateer's Bold Beloved
  (soon)

<u>A Forbidden Love Novella Series</u>
#1 The Wrong Brother
#2 A Brilliant Rose
#3 The Forgotten Wife
#4 An Unwelcome Proposal
#5 Rules to Be Broken
#6 Hearts to Be Broken
#7 Winning her Hand
#8 Conquering her Heart (soon)

Suspenseful Contemporary Romance:

<u>Where There's Love Series</u>
#1 Remember Me

Middle Grade Adventure:

<u>Airborne Trilogy</u>
#1 Fireflies
#2 Butterflies
#3 Dragonflies

Paranormal Fantasy:

<u>Crescent Rock Series</u>
#1 How to Live and Die in Crescent Rock

The Wrong Brother

(#1 A Forbidden Love Novella Series)

by
Bree Wolf

The Wrong Brother

by

Bree Wolf

This is a work of fiction. Names, characters, businesses, places, brands, media, events and incidents are either the products of the author's imagination or used in a fictitious manner.

Any resemblance to actual persons, living or dead, or actual events is purely coincidental.

Cover Art by Victoria Cooper

Copyright © 2016 Sabrina Wolf

www.breewolf.com

ISBN-13: 978-3964820198

To My Sister, Always Know How Much You Mean to Me.

Acknowledgments

My greatest inspiration is still the family that I know I could never do without. As annoying as I know I am during 'editing season', you still remain patient and understanding. Thanks for everything.

Another great contributor, who has earned my eternal gratitude, is Michelle Chenoweth. Her keen eyes spotted all those pesky errors authors are prone to overlook. Thanks a million!

A very special thank-you goes to my avid readers, Monique Takens and Zan-Mari Kiousi, for accompanying me on this journey every step of the way. Your honest feedback and inspiring suggestions proved invaluable.

The Wrong Brother

PROLOGUE

England 1802 (or a variation thereof)

"Argh!" Robert screamed, raking his hands through his hair. "This is agonizing! Why do we have to study Latin if it's a dead language?" Shaking his head, he stared at the pages before him.

"Because it's the language of scholars," Charles replied. "Latin and Greek are at the root of every modern language and help us decipher history long forgotten."

"Ugh!" Robert exclaimed, crinkling his nose as he looked at his younger twin. "You sound just like Mr. Punham." Pushing back his chair, he sat sideways, eyes intent on his brother. "But you know what? There is a reason why history is long forgotten, and that's because it is of no importance. What good will knowing Latin do?"

Putting down his quill, Charles turned to his brother. Although they shared the same coppery brown hair and hazel eyes, the smirk that usually decorated his twin's face spoke volumes of the differences in

11

character they couldn't seem to overcome. "It allows us to read ancient texts and discover how people lived thousands of years ago, what their form of government was, what science they had and—"

"As I said," Robert interrupted, "it is nothing but a waste of time." Lifting his eyes, a longing smile came to his face. "We should be out there." He gestured to the window and the open fields beyond, running all the way to the horizon, only bordered by a thick-growing forest to the east of Bridgemoore Manor. "That's the real world. Adventure awaits out there. This," he gave his book a hard shove so that it went over the edge of the table and hit the floor with a loud *thud*, "this is just boring."

Shaking his head, Charles leaned down and picked up his brother's book. "If you don't study, Father will not let you come to the exhibit at the British Museum."

Robert sighed. "Well, I'd say that would be good news…although going to London would be something. I bet there is a lot going on there apart from dusty museums and such."

"But they have the Rosetta Stone on display," Charles objected, feeling excitement bubble up in his veins. "It is the key to deciphering—"

"Why would I care about some old stone?" Robert whined. "Charles, the world is not only what you find between the covers of your books. It is out there." Rising from his chair, he strode over to the window, an awe-filled expression in his eyes as he gazed at the stretch of green leading from the home he had been born to and the title he was to inherit to adventures unknown. "Let's go," he said, then turned and grabbed his brother's arm.

"Go where?" Charles protested, trying to pull his arm free.

Dragging his brother behind him, Robert yanked open the door then peeked down the corridor. "Let's shoot some arrows," he whispered. When the coast remained clear, he proceeded down the corridor, still holding on to his brother's arm.

"Arrows?" Charles gasped, trying to free himself. "But Father said we were too young. He said—"

"He did when he was our age," Robert objected. "And besides, what could happen?"

"We could get hurt." Unable to wrench himself from his brother's tight grip, Charles reluctantly followed him outside. "How would you know what to do? Have you ever even held a bow and arrow?"

Turning his head, Robert winked at him.

Charles' eyes bulged. "You have? When? Father said—"

"Father is just as much a bookworm as you are," Robert snapped. "I taught myself."

After retrieving a bow as well as a quiver with arrows from a hiding place in the stables, Robert dragged his younger twin toward the tree line, always ducking behind bushes and running from tree to tree so as to stay out of sight.

"Is this truly your idea of fun?" Charles heaved, trying to draw in a deep breath, his face flushed with exertion.

Frowning at his brother, Robert shook his head. "You sound like Aunt Patty, always wheezing as soon as she takes a single step. You should really pull your head out of your books more often and join me in the real world."

Proceeding deeper into the forest, Robert finally stopped at a fallen log. "This is where I come to practice."

Staring at him dumbfounded, Charles shook his head, wondering if this boy, who was just now fitting an arrow into the bow, could truly be his brother.

"This is how you do it," he instructed, eyes concentrated. Never had Charles seen him so focused on anything. "Don't clench your hand. Then pull back the arrow as much as you can, aim a little higher than the target you have your eye on and…," he took a deep breath, "release!"

The arrow shot forward, sailing through the air, and hit its mark—feathers and string tied into a circular pattern hung up in a tree at least fifty yards away.

"Yes!" Robert cheered, hopping up and down in a victory dance. "I told you I could do it!" Then he turned to his brother, and Charles knew that something was up. "Do you want to try?"

Eyes wide, he shook his head.

"Just once," Robert said, holding out his bow. "If you try it, I promise I'll study all afternoon tomorrow."

"Really?" Charles whispered, eyeing the bow and his brother suspiciously. "Only once?"

"Only once."

Reaching out his hand, Charles reluctantly took the bow, surprised how light it was. Then he accepted the arrow his brother offered him and stepped up to the mark. Taking a deep breath, he followed Robert's instructions, carefully fitting the arrow onto the string. Bracing himself, Charles let it slide over his hand as he pulled back the string and took aim.

Beside him, his brother grinned, and Charles felt goose bumps crawl up his back. What had he gotten himself into?

"I promise I'll study with you," Robert said, eyeing his brother with a satisfied grin.

"All right," Charles said and pulled back the arrow as far as he could, feeling beats of sweat pop up on his forehead. His fingers began to tremble with the exertion.

"But only if you hit the mark," Robert whispered into his ear.

"What?" Startled, Charles spun around, staring at his brother, who instantly ducked as the arrow was released and shot past his head through the thicket of the forest.

Staring after it, both brothers winced when a pained howl reached their ears mere moments later.

"Drat!" Robert exclaimed, his hand once more closing around his brother's arm. Dragging him forward, he found his way through the thicket and out of the forest. When the meadow came in sight, voices echoed over from the stables, and they found their tutor, Mr. Punham, lying in the grass, hands wrapped around his left calf, face distorted painfully.

"I hit him," Charles whispered, staring at the arrow protruding from his tutor's lower leg. Blood seeped from the wound, staining his stockings as well as the grass.

Waiting in their father's study, Charles couldn't get the image of Mr. Punham's distorted face out of his head. "I shot him," he whispered for the millionth time. The man had taught him Greek and Latin, opened up the world to him of the beauties of ancient societies, and now, he lay bleeding in the downstairs parlour.

"He will be all right," Robert whispered beside him, his own cheeks a slightly paler colour as well. "After all, it is only a flesh wound."

Staring at him, Charles shook his head. "How can you say that? How can you—?"

The door opened, and both boys shot to their feet.

Never had Charles given his father cause for displeasure, and so when the man's stern eyes fell on him, Charles felt tears stinging his eyes. "I am so sorry," he whispered, eyes fixed on the floor.

Coming to stand before them, their father shook his head. "I am severely disappointed in you." His voice rang cold, not resembling the kind-hearted man Charles knew him to be. "I might have expected such behaviour from you, Robert, but Charles, what in the devil's name has gotten into you? Shooting an arrow at your tutor?" Again, he shook his head, disbelief darkening his eyes. "I thought you to be a responsible, young man, not a reckless child." Sighing, he closed his eyes. "I suppose I was mistaken."

His gaze shifting from one son to the other, Viscount Norwood crossed his arms, and Charles knew that he was about to find out what punishment he was to receive. "Since I cannot trust that you will display appropriate manners when in London, I am afraid I have no choice but to leave you here." Charles gasped, feeling the blood rush from his head. "You are to stay at Bridgemoore under Mr. Punham's strict supervision—should he decide to stay on—and spend your summer reviewing the appropriate behaviour of a gentleman. Am I understood?"

"Yes, Father," Charles whispered as stars began to dance before his eyes and the breath caught in his throat. "I am so sorry."

"Well, it is a bit late for—"

"Father!" Robert interrupted, taking a step forward. "Charles is not at fault here; I am."

Unable to believe his ears, Charles stared at his brother.

Lord Norwood's eyes narrowed. "What do you mean? Did Charles not shoot the arrow? When we came upon you, he was holding the bow in his hand."

Straightening to his full height, Robert raised his head. "He took it from me. In fact, the only reason he was out there was to try to stop me. It was my idea. The bow and arrows are mine as well. I have been practising for a while now, and when Charles found out, he told me I was not to continue. However, I did not listen." He took a deep breath. "I know I should have. I did not mean to hurt Mr. Punham. It was an accident." He glanced at his brother. "Do not punish him. He is merely trying to protect me."

For a moment, Lord Norwood remained silent, glancing back and forth between his sons, his eyes narrowed with suspicion. "Is that true?" he finally asked, looking at Charles.

Feeling the blood drain from his face once more, Charles didn't know what to say. He glanced at his brother, stammering unintelligibly.

Nodding his head imperceptibly, Robert's eyes urged him to agree.

"Well, I..." He took a deep breath and then looked at his father. "Yes, it is."

"I see." For a moment, Lord Norwood's eyes lingered on his younger son before they moved to Robert. "In this case, it is you who will remain at Bridgemoore for the summer, and you will remain indoors and study." Robert swallowed. "You do not set a foot outside, am I understood?"

Robert drew in a sharp breath before nodding his head. "Yes, father."

Returning to the seat behind his desk, Lord Norwood bid them to leave. "Oh, and Charles? Although it is noble to want to protect your brother, I would strongly advise against lying to your father! Is that clear?"

Charles nodded, then followed his brother out into the hall. The second the door closed behind them, he pulled Robert back. "Why did you do that? It was my fault. I shot Mr. Punham."

Robert shrugged. "That may be so, but the only reason you were out there was because I did not give you a choice."

"That's not true," Charles disagreed. "I could have just left. You did not force me to pick up the bow."

"Maybe not, but I distracted you." When Charles opened his mouth to protest, Robert lifted a hand to stop him. "Leave it be, Charles. Go to London, see that stupid stone of yours, and who knows, a day may come when I need you to protect me." Smiling, Robert clamped a hand on his brother's shoulder then turned around and walked down the corridor.

Charles simply stared after him, for the first time understanding the true meaning of brotherhood.

1

A BROTHER'S RETURN

Fifteen Years Later

reathing in the early night air, Robert Dashwood looked up at the looming structure of Bridgemoore Manor. It had been years since he had been here. Not since his father had died and passed on his title to him.

The very sight of his childhood home made his insides quiver. Memories resurfaced of careless days spent in leisure with his brother, with his friends. A smile drew up the corners of his mouth as he remembered the many days he had spent in detention, punishment for yet another reckless deed he had felt compelled to do. Those days had been good; yet, the moment he had come of age, Robert had left, his feet trembling with the need to get away and see the world.

Title or no, Robert knew that if it hadn't been for Charles' note, he would never have come home.

Climbing the front stairs with long strides, he entered the house, silence hanging like cobwebs in every corner. At least as children, their own voices had sent echoes through the house. Now, it lay almost dead, like one of Charles' old, dusty books.

Knowing with absolute certainty where he would find his brother, Robert made his way across the marble hall and down the west corridor until he reached his father's old study. Again, a rueful smile came to his face. How many times had he stood outside these very doors waiting for his father to call him inside and shake his head at him for yet another unwise decision?

But, not today.

His hand only hesitating for a moment, Robert slid open the door and stepped inside, his careful footsteps all but silent on the parquet floor. After his eyes had adjusted to the rather dim light, he found himself staring across the room at his father's old desk, his brother sitting in its leather armchair, quill in hand, head bent over some papers.

For a moment, Robert just looked at him, a smile curling his lips. In a strange way, he felt transported through time as though he was a young boy again, and the man behind the desk was his father. While Charles and his father had always shared the basic characteristics of their personality, Robert had often felt like an outsider to their shared interests. Never had he been able to relate to what brought them such joy.

Still, he felt a deep connection to his brother, and for the first time, Robert was glad he had come home.

"Squint anymore, and I'm sure you'll go blind."

At the sound of his voice, Charles' head snapped up, his eyes growing wide as he beheld his mirror image standing by the door. "Robert!" he exclaimed, almost jumping to his feet. Rounding the desk, a delighted smile on his face, Charles came toward him. "A part of me thought you wouldn't come," he said, drawing him into his arms. "It is so good to see you."

For a moment, Robert closed his eyes, savouring his brother's embrace and all the emotions it elicited. Then he stood back. "You cannot truly believe I would miss my little brother getting married. What sort of man do you take me for?"

"The worst kind." Shaking his head, Charles laughed. "Look at you! You look like a pirate. When was the last time you cut your hair?"

Compared to Charles' rather stylish crop, Robert wore his auburn hair long and tied in the back, a perfect match to his loose-fitting clothes. "What can I say? I have a reputation to uphold."

Charles laughed. "Do I dare ask what you have been doing?"

"I'm sure you don't want to know."

"I suppose you're right," Charles admitted. "Frankly, your escapades are well known all over London. Did you know they've earned you the rather flattering nickname of 'Notorious Norwood'?" Again, Charles shook his head; an amused smile seemed to tickle the corners of his mouth. "I generally tend to turn a deaf ear."

"That sounds like a good idea," Robert confirmed, not daring to be any more specific. If his brother only knew half of what he had done, he would have turned deep red at the very sight of him. Maybe London knew a lot less than it thought. "So? You're getting married tomorrow. Isn't that a bit soon?" He winked at his brother. "Is there a reason you're rushing this wedding?"

Charles shook his head at him again. To Robert, it seemed like all Charles ever did was shake his head at him. "I'd appreciate it if you would refrain from any such comments with regard to my fiancée. For your information, we have been engaged since last season. Was it my fault I had such trouble tracking you down? You have not changed in the least."

"I saw no need." A devilish smile drew up the corners of his mouth, and Robert saw its effects on his brother's face long before he spoke again. "After all, in my experience the ladies generally do not merely want the saint, but a little bit of the sinner as well." He shrugged, enjoying the slightly shocked expression on his brother's face. "And you know me, I hate to disappoint."

Slowly, the shock fell from Charles' face and was replaced by a rather indulgent smile. Once again, Robert felt like a young boy being called into his father's study. "You truly have not changed," his brother repeated. Turning to the liquor cabinet, he filled two glasses, offering one to him.

Downing it in one gulp, Robert cleared his throat. "So? Who is the lucky woman?" he asked, feeling the need to change the subject.

"Lady Isabella Carrington."

"Lord Gadbury's daughter?"

Charles nodded. "The eldest."

"I don't believe I've had the pleasure of meeting her." Pouring himself another drink, Robert settled into one of the armchairs by the window front, gesturing for his brother to follow. "Tell me about her."

Taking a seat, Charles smiled. "She is indeed very amiable and possesses all the qualities of a lady."

Robert chuckled. "You truly sound enthusiastic, brother. How did you meet?"

"At the British Museum."

Robert groaned, hearing his worst fears realised.

"She, too, was engrossed with the most recent Egyptian arte-facts," Charles elaborated, a slightly disapproving look in his eyes as he looked at his brother.

"This truly sounds like a love match," Robert teased, unable to stop himself.

Lips pressed into a thin line, Charles eyed him with displeasure. "And what would you know about love? Believe me, although I tried not to, it has been nearly impossible not to know how you've spent the last few years. More than once, I've heard the whispers that follow you. From what I can gather, you've never spent more than a few days in the company of one woman."

Again, Robert chuckled as memories surfaced that would have Charles faint on the spot. "Yes, but I always thought you were differ-ent. As dedicated as you are to your dusty, old books, I always thought that one day, you'd find a woman you'd be equally dedicated to. In-stead, you seem to have found one who shares your dedication to…," he gestured at the tall bookcases lining the far wall of the study, "those." This time, it was Robert who shook his head at his brother. "Quite frankly, I can't wait to meet her. She seems to be your other half."

Downing his drink, Charles set down the glass with a loud *clank*. "What do you want, Robert? Certainly, even you can see the ad-vantage in choosing one's wife based on common interests. You can't truly believe that to be wrong?"

Seeing the pulse hammering in his brother's throat, Robert lifted his hands in a gesture of truce. "Far be it from me to oppose your match." Leaning forward, he rested his elbows on his knees, his eyes focused on his brother's face. "But to be frank, you sound more taken with the old Egyptian trinkets than your future wife. The real question is does she get your heart pounding?"

Charles huffed. "In what way is that relevant?"

Robert laughed. "If she did, you'd know why." Clearing his throat, Robert took a swig from his glass. "I really did not mean any disrespect but was merely curious what kind of woman had captured your attention."

Looking rather annoyed, Charles eyed him carefully. "She is well-read in history, which means we are never at a loss for words in the other's company. Also, her demeanour speaks of a courteous and noble character, and she will, I am certain, represent our family with grace. Even though she is a few years younger than I am, she is not childish in the least but behaves with the utmost respect toward anyone in her presence. Upon meeting her, I am certain you will believe so yourself."

"Dear Brother, I never meant to suggest that she was not worthy of our family or of you." All teasing left Robert's voice, and his eyes became serious as they looked into his brother's. "I simply meant to ensure that you have indeed chosen wisely."

"Wisely, brother? And what would you know of choosing a wife?" Charles laughed, once more shaking his head. "Am I mistaken, or are you still looking for the future Lady Norwood?"

Robert chuckled. The mere thought seemed ludicrous. "I have no intention of ever marrying. I thought you knew that."

"You cannot be serious," Charles objected, quite honestly stunned by his brother's words. "What about your title? You need an heir."

"An heir?" Robert laughed. The life that his parents had lived, the life that Charles and his new bride were about to embark upon was the very life that would have him running for the hills within a few days. He was not made for a settled life. He knew that, and he wouldn't do anyone any favours if he pretended differently. "Why would I worry about an heir? There are much more important and, quite frankly, much more amusing things in life." He winked at Charles, who looked almost scandalised. "And besides, I always thought you'd make a much better viscount than I ever could."

Again, Charles stared at him, for a moment too stunned to say anything. "You cannot be serious?"

Robert shrugged, the need to lighten the mood tucking up the corners of his mouth. "I rarely am. However, today I'll make an exception."

"Robert, you cannot—"

"Let's not talk about this anymore. In a few days, I'll be gone again. Let us enjoy what time we have together." Rising from his chair, Robert refilled his drink. "To you and your perfect match," he said, raising his glass. "I wish you all the happiness in the world, Charles. If anyone deserves it, it is you. I am sure you chose well, and that she will make you happy."

A touched smile playing on his lips, Charles approached him. "Thank you. This means a lot to me."

"You're welcome, Brother."

2

A PERFECT MATCH

Seeing her own face in the mirror, Isabella sighed. As her eyes travelled downward, taking in the elegant wedding dress that had once been her mother's, a small lump settled in her throat, and her hands began to tremble.

Today was the day.

Her wedding day.

After all her careful planning, she was finally here. She had found the man who would make her a fine husband, who would respect and honour her, who cared about her mind as much as he cared about her heart. A man she could share her passion for history with, who knew well the desire to understand foreign cultures and who she could spend entire afternoons with, their noses hidden in a book and enjoy the peaceful silence that simply existed between two like-minded people. Did he ever dream of travelling to these foreign places like she did? Isabella wondered. She didn't know, but there would be plenty of time to find that out.

She had chosen well.

"Why are you marrying him?" Adriana's voice cut into Isabella's musings. "He is so dull."

"Shush," their mother chided. "This is your sister's wedding day. Do not ruin it for her."

From the corner of her eye, Isabella saw Adriana take a step back, shaking her head. She all but felt her sister's disapproving eyes glide over her as though she had agreed to marry her worst enemy. "If you think him dull, you must think me dull as well," she said, trying to ignore the sting her sister's words had caused. "And yet, it would only prove that we suit each other."

For a long moment, Adriana didn't say a word. Nonetheless, Isabella's skin began to crawl as though she was just about to be found out and revealed a liar; as if her sister's eyes could see through her outer shell and into her core.

A place not even Isabella dared to look.

"There," her mother whispered, dropping the veil she had been working on. "You can hardly see where it was ripped." A radiant smile on her face, her mother looked over Isabella's shoulder, meeting her eyes in the mirror. "You are a most beautiful bride, *mi corazón.*"

Turning to face her mother, Isabella felt her own lips curl up. "Thank you for everything." Hugging her mother tight, she met her sister's calculating gaze and closed her eyes determined to ignore it.

Stepping back, her mother dabbed her eyes. "I'd better go and see to your father." She gazed at her daughter, and her eyes once more took on a dream-like expression like someone lost in a memory, seeing something no one else could, and the corners of her mouth pulled up into a smile. "How beautiful you are," she whispered before she turned and left the room.

The moment the door closed behind their mother, Adriana came to life. "I implore you, Isabella, think about what you're doing. He is not the right man for you."

Isabella sighed, praying for strength. "You've been saying this for weeks now. Why won't you understand? He quite obviously is not the right man for you, but he is for me. Why can you not accept that?" Looking at Adriana, Isabella tried to glimpse what had caused her sister's stern insistence that marrying Charles was a mistake; for the longer it lasted the more rattled Isabella felt. "Please explain to me why you think he is not the right man for me!" she asked, feeling the last bit of patience slip through her fingers. "You cannot possibly be speaking from personal experience for I do not see a ring on your finger."

An indulgent smile on her face, Adriana shook her head. "And you won't until I find it."

"It?" Isabella asked, avoiding her sister's eyes by busying herself with arranging and re-arranging her skirt. This discussion made her quite uncomfortable—as always.

"Love," Adriana whispered as if there could be no question. "True love. The kind Mother and Father have."

Isabella snorted. "Do not be absurd."

Brows drawn down, Adriana stepped toward her. "You do not believe that Mother and Father share a true love?"

Isabella shrugged. "I believe they love each other. I do. Yet, I can count the couples that I have seen gazing upon each other the way Mother and Father do on one hand." Meeting her sister's eyes, she shook her head. "The love they have is rare. What are the odds of all of us finding it in a mere lifetime? No, I'd rather marry a man I can respect, a man who is a friend, than wait for someone who may not even exist?"

"Who may not even exist?" Adriana echoed, a look of bewilderment on her face. "Have you never felt it? Not once?"

"Felt what? A mild infatuation that cools as soon as the sun rises on the next day?" Isabella smiled at her little sister. "No, I've made my choice. You cannot sway me from my path."

"I only hope you will not come to regret it," Adriana whispered. "For even these mild infatuations as you call them have the strength to set your world on fire even if it is just for a day or a week. And besides, how do you know they'll cool? Who knows? Maybe one day, you will meet someone special, and the very sight of him will turn your knees into pudding and set free an armada of butterflies in your belly. What if that happens and you find yourself married already? What will you do then?"

Feeling a lump settle in her stomach, Isabella drew a deep breath. She loved her little sister dearly; yet, her misguided, overly romanticised notion of love was trying on most days. However, today, Isabella felt her own resolve weaken, and doubts steal into her heart and mind. What if…?

No! She called herself to reason. She had made her choice, and she would see it through. After all, what kind of a woman would accept a man's marriage proposal only to retract it the very day of her wedding? She would be ruined as would her family. Even if her sister were to find the man of her dreams, his family might not approve of the match because of the damage her own refusal to marry Charles had caused. What would Adriana say then?

"I will honour my marriage vows," Isabella finally said, sitting down on the settee, her trembling hands hidden in the folds of her skirt. "Charles is a wonderful man. You might consider him dull, but to me, he is the answer to my prayers."

"He is?" Adriana asked, taking a seat beside her sister. "How can that be if you hold no love for him?"

"I care for him deeply, and I believe that as time goes on I will come to care for him a little more each day." Isabella smiled, feeling the effect of her own words on her heart. A comforting warmth spread through her, and she took a deep breath, feeling herself relax. "You know how we met, do you not?"

Adriana nodded.

"I have met many men who believe that a woman's mind is not capable of rational thought, at least, not in the same way a man's is." Isabella shook her head, remembering the many conversations she'd had with men that had made her feel as though she was an empty vessel with no thoughts of her own. "Whenever I speak my mind, these men do not listen or—what might be worse—ignore what I say. They do not care who I am. Their interest never goes below the surface."

Remembering, a smile tucked at the corners of her mouth. "Charles was different. From the very day we met, he seemed elated to have found someone he could share his thoughts with, someone he could talk to about what he cared about and have that someone understand how deeply he felt about it." Taking her sister's hand, Isabella met her eyes. "I felt the same way. We are a match."

Adriana took a deep breath, and Isabella could see some of the determination to argue leave her body. "I never meant to say that he was not a good man," her sister relented. "I do remember how happy you always looked whenever you met him at an event and how you would spend most of your time talking about dead civilisations." Adriana grinned, shaking her head, and Isabella couldn't help but laugh. "However, I cannot help but wonder if that is enough to make you happy for the rest of your days. Is he truly the man you want to marry? Or is he a man you are afraid to lose if you do not marry him?"

"Of course, I do not want to lose him." Isabella struggled to find the words to make her sister understand how Charles made her feel. "Without him, I feel incomplete as though something is missing; something vital that I cannot do without."

"Are you certain?" Adriana asked. "I mean, I can see that you care about him. A lot. Still, the way you spoke of him makes me think that what you cherish about him is his friendship. From what I can tell, he is a good friend. Maybe the only true friend you ever had, and, of course, you cherish him, but is it enough? Enough for a marriage? For you to be his wife?" Adriana shook her head. "What if being husband and wife ruins the friendship you have built? What if neither one of you can go beyond? In your mind, yes, but not where your hearts are concerned."

Eyeing her younger sister carefully, Isabella frowned. "I am not repulsed by his touch if that is what you are suggesting?"

Adriana chuckled. "Not repulsed? Is that truly your idea of a good marriage? Of the man you intend to invite into your bed?" She shook her head. "Have you truly never felt even the smallest shred of passion? Are you so determined to live without it for the rest of your life?"

Feeling a slight blush creep up her cheeks, Isabella rose to her feet. Not sure what to say or do, she strode over to the window, keeping her eyes fixed on the beautiful gardens of Bridgemoore. Frankly, Isabella had never contemplated the idea of what it would be like to share her husband's bed. It was a stipulation of marriage, and as far as she knew, all couples somehow managed this aspect of their union.

Remembering the many dances they had shared over the course of their engagement as well as before, Isabella knew the lightness of his touch. With delicate hands, he had guided her across the floor, his skin feeling warm against her own. In addition, she recalled him assisting her into a carriage countless times, giving her a chance to feel the strength beneath his gentle touch. One night a mere few weeks ago when they had walked the gardens after a ball held at Bridgemoore, he had brushed a strand of her raven-black hair from her face, his finger lightly skimming her cheek. Even remembering that night, a delicate tingle went through her, and she smiled.

Yes, she had chosen well. Charles was the man for her, whether or not her sister understood.

3

VOWS SPOKEN

Bridgemoore's chapel sat nestled between a grove of maples, a bushy hedge running all the way to the main building. The sun touched the ground with soft hands, its light glistening in the morning dew clinging to the long-stemmed grass, which grew in abundance in the many meadows on the estate.

Smiling faces met her when Isabella stepped outside, her father's steady arm guiding her trembling feet. He patted her hand and looked down at her, his eyes shining with a hint of tears. "You are such a beautiful bride," he whispered. "Just like your mother."

"Thank you, Father." Taking a deep breath, she set one foot before the other, feeling the rest of the procession follow them down the small path to the chapel.

This was it. Her day had come. Isabella felt a nervous tremble run all the way from her head down to her toes. Had Adriana's words shaken her resolve after all?

Nonsense! Even though she cared for Charles and felt certain that a future with him held nothing but joy, it still was a crossroads.

Bridgemoore was her new home now, and in a matter of days, her parents as well as Adriana would return home to Elmsmore. The thought of not seeing them every day brought a lump to her throat that she couldn't quite dislodge, no matter how hard she tried. It was the dark cloud on an otherwise sunny day.

Entering the chapel, Isabella's eyes were instantly drawn to the front where her future husband stood waiting, a gentle smile on his face. When he beheld her, his eyes lit up, and the lump in her throat vanished.

Yes, he was, indeed, the one.

After everyone had taken their seats, her father slowly led her down the aisle. When they had reached the front, he kissed her on the forehead, smiling down at her with wet eyes. "I am so happy for you," he whispered, yet, Isabella could feel a hint of reluctance as he placed her hand in her future husband's.

Taking a deep breath, she smiled at her father, reaching out with her other hand and squeezing his. "Thank you."

As the priest began his usual litany, Isabella found her eyes travelling to her husband. She saw the kind smile that played on his lips, and the affection that shone in his eyes whenever they met hers. Nevertheless, he too seemed to be afflicted by a certain nervousness for Isabella also felt a slight tremble run through his arm and travel into her own.

Yes, they were indeed a perfect match.

Slowly, she felt her heart calm itself and the tremble in her arms and legs subside, and before long, the ceremony was over. Turning toward her, Charles took both her hands, then leaned down and gave her a soft kiss on the lips.

It was soft and sweet, and the last shred of Isabella's doubts vanished into thin air.

Turning to a cheering crowd, her eyes swept across the many people who had come to celebrate this day with them. Her mother was crying, dabbing a handkerchief to her eyes, one arm wrapped around her father's arm. He, too, had a tear running down his cheek but quickly brushed it away. When their eyes met, he nodded his head. Even Adriana had a smile on her face.

Deep down, Isabella had expected a worried frown or even an angry scowl from Adriana. Nevertheless, whatever her doubts, Adriana had decided to put them away and allow her sister to enjoy her wedding. Whatever the reason, Isabella was grateful.

Smiling, she glanced at her husband. Here she was, among the people she loved the most, and she couldn't be happier.

Unexpectedly, a sense of being watched came over Isabella, which considering the circumstances was not unusual, and yet, her eyes swept over the crowd looking for the ones that had sent a shiver down her back.

The instant she found them, her heart stopped.

Hazel eyes stared back into hers—the same eyes she had seen looking into hers countless times. However, these eyes were different. They had a darker edge to them reminding her of a raging fire burning underneath, instead of a gentle flame.

Blinking, Isabella tried to focus, forcing her gaze away from the man's eyes. However, looking at his face only increased her unrest. Feeling her heart hammering in her chest, Isabella knew who he was. She knew not only his eyes, but also his face, his stature. She had seen them many times in the man by her side. Who else could share those traits but the twin brother she had yet to meet? The notorious twin whose escapades were known all over London?

"Are you all right, my dear?" Charles asked beside her. "You look pale. Do you need some air?" Seeing the weak smile on her face, he did not wait for an answer but, instead, led her through the throng of people and out into the light.

Breathing in the fresh morning air, Isabella felt her nerves steady as though of their own accord. Her heart, however, was still in an uproar, and when the man that shared her husband's eyes suddenly came toward them, her whole world turned upside down.

Everything Isabella thought she knew was proved false. Always had her mind triumphed over her heart. However, now in this very moment as she found herself shamelessly gazing into his eyes, her heart beat in her chest so strongly that she could not ignore it any longer. Who was her perfect match?

Her heart and mind strongly disagreed, and to Isabella's great dismay, it was her heart that came out the victor. The battle was swift and short-lived; so short-lived in fact that Isabella hardly noticed what was going on.

She took a shallow breath, trying desperately to stop the shaking in her legs, and all of a sudden found herself staring in the face of love.

What if you meet your true love and you find yourself married already? What will you do then? Her sister's words echoed in her mind, and Isa-

bella closed her eyes, willing the flutter in her heart to stop. Her attempts, however, were futile, and as she opened them again, she found herself looking at the man who held her heart.

"Robert!" Charles exclaimed. "When I did not see you this morning, I was worried you'd sleep through the ceremony."

"Nothing in the world would make me miss my little brother's wedding," the man said, his voice, a little raspy and yet oddly melodious, touched her very core, and Isabella felt her hands begin to tremble.

After greeting his brother, Robert turned his eyes to her, and in an instant, the whole world fell away.

For a long moment, Isabella forgot her husband's presence, their guests' voices no longer reached her ear, and she could not feel the morning sun warming her face.

As his gaze burned into hers, Isabella almost gasped when his hand touched hers in a formal greeting. Just like his eyes, his touch ignited a fire within her that completely took her breath away. Feeling paralysed, she watched as he bent his head, his fiery hair so long that he could tie it in the back, and kissed her hand.

The second his lips touched her skin, Isabella was sure she would faint. Only her husband's steady arm held her upright.

That thought brought a deep blush to her cheeks, and she quickly averted her eyes lest she do something even more scandalous.

What was going on? Who was this man? And why did he make her feel so…?

Again, her gaze shifted upward, daring a glance at the enigmatic eyes that had so captured her soul.

Fortunately, he was conversing with her husband, his attention currently focused elsewhere. Taking a deep breath, Isabella eyed him from under her lashes.

Indeed, they did look remarkably alike. From a distance, the only thing telling them apart was the difference in clothing as well as the length of their hair. While her husband looked like the perfect gentleman, neatly dressed, hair trimmed and in order, his brother had a more casual air about him. Even wearing clothes of the same style, he still seemed to rebel against formal etiquette as his collar was unbuttoned, no cravat in sight.

However, on a closer look, they seemed like fire and water, or rather like a hearth fire and a raging wild fire. Charles was passionate; she knew him to be, and yet, his passion was of a more gentle nature.

His brother, on the other hand, appeared wild and untameable as though not even he knew what he would do the next day.

Why do you care? A voice whispered in the back of her head.

I don't, Isabella objected, knowing it to be a lie, yet, unable to admit to it.

At the wedding breakfast, Robert could barely eat a morsel. Although he hadn't eaten since the previous night, he did not dare think about food. His stomach was in knots, and whenever his gaze travelled to his brother and his new bride, more were added. Twisting and turning, they felt like they were about to rip his insides out.

Moaning under his breath, he reached for his wine glass, downing its contents in one gulp. *This won't do*, he thought and reached for the bottle.

Shaking his head, he closed his eyes, and the second he did, he found Isabella's dark brown eyes gazing into his.

His head snapped up, and he almost tore his eyes open, only to find himself staring across the table at the very woman who had turned his world upside down in a single second.

Inhaling deeply, he swallowed and then quickly excused himself before he could do something stupid.

The rest of the morning, Robert spent in the corner of Bridgemoore's enormous hall, watching his brother, or rather his brother's bride, like a predator about to strike. He knew it was wrong; yet, he could not help himself.

Was this truly the woman his brother had spoken to him about the night before? After everything Charles had told him, he had imagined her…differently. He had thought her a typical wallflower, timid and shy, her nose constantly in a book, the real world only glanced at as though it was a monster threatening to swallow her up if she dared meet its eyes.

But Isabella was different.

Of course, he hardly knew her. Still, from the many glimpses he had stolen of her, Robert felt certain that a passionate nature rested beneath her somewhat rigid exterior. While her father looked like the typical English gentleman, rather fair skin in tone with light brown hair, her mother, on the other hand, seemed to have her origins somewhere

in the European south. Her hair was as black as the night, even darker than Isabella's, and her skin had a rich olive tone to it that increased Robert's impression of an unusual match. Where had old Lord Gatsby met his wife?

Shaking his head, Robert refocused his thoughts on Isabella. She looked nothing like her father; on the contrary, she shared her mother's southern flair. Only her eyes held a hint of unease, that her mother's lacked. She hardly dared look at him. However, when their eyes did meet, she quickly turned her head away, a deep flush creeping up her cheeks. Why was she embarrassed? Was he not the only one to experience these emotions?

Unable to stop himself, Robert approached the happy couple when they left the floor after their first dance together. Taking a deep breath, he forced a nonchalant smile on his face and once more congratulated his brother on his marriage.

"Thank you, Robert." Nodding his head, Charles glanced at his bride, her hand resting in the crook of his arm, his hand covering hers.

Robert felt sick to the stomach. He had to fight for composure lest he slap away his brother's hand for daring to touch her. The insanity of this thought felt like a punch to the gut, and Robert was certain the whole world, or at the very least his brother, could read his struggle clearly on his face.

Still fighting for composure, he swallowed the lump in his throat and turned to Isabella. "Our father would have welcomed you into the family with open arms," Robert forced out through gritted teeth. Out of the corner of his eye, he noticed a delighted smile spread over his brother's face, and guilt settled in his stomach, adding to his misery. "Let me do so on his behalf. You make a beautiful bride, and I am certain you will make my brother a wonderful wife." Again, his insides twisted into knots, and he almost groaned in agony.

A shy smile began on her face, and her eyes barely met his. "Thank you, my lord. You are most kind."

"Please, call me Robert. After all, we are family now." He knew he shouldn't, and yet, the desperate need to touch her, feel her skin against his, won over his sense of propriety. Glancing at his brother, he asked, "May I have this dance?"

While Charles' face betrayed nothing but true delight, his new bride looked rather shocked. For a moment, her eyes opened wide as though the mere thought terrified her. However, she made an effort to control her fear and with a rather uneasy smile took his offered hand.

At her touch, a raging fire rolled through him, scorching his insides and igniting a passion so deep, he all but gulped for air. Uncertain whether or not he had just made the biggest mistake of his life, Robert led her back to the dance floor where a country dance had just begun. Finding their places, he reluctantly let go of her hand, experiencing the absence of her soft touch as the greatest loss of his life.

As they moved to the music in line with the other couples, Robert could not keep his eyes off Isabella, at the same time noticing that she in turn didn't dare look at him. "My brother tells me you read a lot."

"I do, yes," she whispered; her eyes, however, remained cast down.

"What do you read?" he asked, desperately trying to make her talk while keeping his feet in time to the music. Nothing in his life had ever been more challenging.

"History mostly."

Had he misjudged her? Robert wondered. Was she a timid wallflower after all? Why would she not look at him?

"So does Charles," he mumbled, realising for the first time that his brother might have chosen well after all. Had his heart so deceived him? However, he could still feel the flame her touch had ignited burn strongly within him. Was he going mad?

"Yes, he does."

"Well,...," he all but stammered, grasping at straws. "I have never been fond of books myself," he admitted. "They paint a rather empty picture of the world. I always prefer to see these place with my own eyes."

Unexpectedly, her gaze shifted from somewhere beyond his shoulder and focused on his face. "You travel, my lord?" she breathed, a tentative smile lighting up her beautiful features. "Out-outside of England?"

Delighted with her sudden interest, Robert nodded. "Mostly, yes. I've spent my youth in England—due to my father's wishes—but now, I want to see the world." As he watched the pulse in her neck quicken, Robert felt his own join the rhythm hers had set.

As though out of breath, she beamed at him, a sparkle in her eyes he had not seen before. "Where have you travelled?"

Exhaling slowly, Robert smiled. "Countless places, and yet, there are still so many I need to see. I want to see the Chinese Wall, the

canals of Venice, the stone city of Petra in Jordan, the Egyptian pyramids—"

"The pyramids," she gasped, awe shining in her eyes. "I've always wanted to see them."

"I'm sure they would love for you to visit." Transfixed by the passion lurking just beneath the surface, Robert barely noticed that the music stopped.

Offering her his arm, he led her to the refreshment table. Although she still seemed a little shaken, her earlier shyness had vanished. "So, you do not intend to stay at Bridgemoore?" she asked, accepting a glass of wine from him.

"No, I merely came to see my brother married," he admitted, almost forgetting to whom he was speaking. As though mirroring his own feelings, she averted her eyes at his words, a slight blush colouring her cheeks.

"I am certain he will be sorry to see you leave so soon," she mumbled, hopeful eyes glancing back up into his.

"Maybe I can extend my stay," he whispered, feeling the blood boil in his veins. What was he doing? She was his brother's wife! How could he betray him?

"Ah, there you are." At Charles' voice, Isabella flinched just as much as Robert did himself, and more guilt seeped into his heart. What was he doing to her? Did she feel the same way? Had he stolen her heart as she had stolen his? A heart that now by all rights belonged to his brother?

Slapping him on the back, Charles laughed. "I see you have not completely forgotten Mr. Punham's instructions! Although I did catch you stumble here and there."

Charles had watched them dance? Robert thought, an iron fist squeezing his heart. If he had seen him stumble, had he also seen...? Seen what? They had only talked. Nothing had happened. Yet, Robert's heart knew this to be a lie.

This ought to have been the happiest day of her life, Isabella thought, watching her new husband from across the room. Instead, guilt and a feeling of utter hopelessness tormented her heart and soul.

As she watched him laughing and jesting with friends he had known since his school days at Eton, her heart sank. He was such a wonderful man! He had so many endearing qualities, which truly made him her perfect match!

Then why couldn't she stop herself from scanning the crowd for his brother?

"Looking for someone?"

Startled, Isabella spun around and found herself mesmerised by the same hazel eyes that had smiled at her only a moment ago from across the room. Only these eyes held something deeper, something she could not quite name. As they stared into hers, the breath caught in her throat, and she reached out for the wall beside her in order to steady herself.

"Are you all right?" Robert asked, extending a hand to offer support. However, before his hand touched her elbow, he thought better of it. "Should I fetch Charles?"

"No." Isabella shook her head, afraid to meet his eyes. "I am fine. It's just...the excitement."

A smile playing on his lips, he leaned a shoulder against the wall, his head slightly angled toward hers. "Charles truly knows how to throw a party like no one else does."

Understanding his statement for what it was, Isabella laughed, feeling the tension in her shoulders subside. "He would prefer a good book, I am sure."

"He would," Robert agreed, and the smile slowly slid off his face as his eyes looked into hers. "He is a good man and a wonderful brother. Despite my...shortcomings, he has always looked out for me. He has always protected me even when I couldn't appreciate it at the time."

Isabella nodded. "He is loyal. He would never break a promise once given." Tears formed in the corners of her eyes, and she took a deep breath.

An anguished expression came to his face as he watched her. "Isabella, I..."

Fighting the sob rising in her throat, Isabella swallowed and for a second closed her eyes. When she opened them again, a single tear spilled over and ran down her cheek.

As though he had no control over his limbs, Robert's hand reached toward her face. Gently cupping her cheek, his thumb skimmed over her skin, brushing away the tear.

For a moment, his hand lingered, and Isabella held her breath.

Then, as though slapped, he withdrew it, nervously glancing around. "I apologise. I shouldn't have done that." Shaking his head, he looked at her. "I should go before…" Nevertheless, he stayed. His feet didn't move, and neither did his eyes leave her face. "Charles is lucky to have found you." Gritting his teeth, he took a slow and painful breath. "I am certain you will find him a good husband, and I wish you all the happiness in the world." He slightly bowed his head at her, a longing smile flashing over his face before he turned and walked away.

Forcing herself to remain where she was, Isabella stared after him as her heart broke into a million pieces with each step he took.

4

A MOMENT OF TRUTH

ong after the music had stopped and the guests had taken their leave, Robert sat in the ballroom, a glass that seemed to refill itself as if by magic in his hand. Not one to chastise him, Robert quickly downed its contents again and again, not daring to think about what he was doing, much less what his brother and his new bride were doing at this very moment.

And yet, despite his best efforts, images would float into his mind, tormenting his soul in a way he had never thought possible.

What had happened that day? Who was that woman? How did she have such power over him?

Only this morning, he had awoken, delighted to spend a few days in his brother's company, see his childhood home again and then return to his travels. He hadn't even made up his mind where to go next. He never did. He never made plans. He always went where the winds would take him, ending up in places he had never thought to visit.

And now, he was sitting in the dark, working his way to a drunken stupor, which he would regret come morning, and sulking over the sick sense of humour fate obviously had.

Notorious Norwood had finally fallen in love, and as if that wasn't ridiculous enough, it was with his brother's wife for God's sakes. How could he? How was this possible? It had taken all but one look into her dark brown eyes, and he had lost his heart to her. Never in a million years would he have thought this possible!

As he reached for his glass again, footsteps echoed over from the doorway, and Robert spun around, almost losing his footing as the room began to spin. "Who's there?" he drawled, hands gripping the table top.

"Drinking in the dark," Charles observed, approaching the table. "What happened, Robert?" His eyes narrowed as he took in his brother's miserable condition. "This is not you. Tell me what is going on."

Chuckling, Robert returned his attention to the drink in his hand. "What are you doing here? Do you not have something better to…do? Or are you already tired of marriage?"

Pulling out a chair, Charles sat down, his forehead creased in concern. "Lady Gadbury and Adriana are tending to Isabella in her bedchamber. I do not wish to intrude too soon, so…," he took a deep breath, and his nose crinkled as he smelled the stench of liquor emanating from his brother. "Talk to me, Robert. What has you acting like this?"

Your wife, Robert thought. *The fact that she is* your *wife!*

Instead, he mumbled, "Nothing. I am just celebrating my return." Lifting his glass, he toasted his brother before once more downing its contents in a single gulp.

Yanking the glass from his grip, Charles stared at him. "For God's sake, Robert, what has happened? Last night, you were in such high spirits. Nothing suggested this kind of misery you suddenly seem to find yourself in."

Yesterday, I was happily oblivious!

"Robert, please!"

Hearing the worry in his brother's voice, Robert took a deep breath. "It is nothing for you to concern yourself." Forcing a smile on his face, he turned to look at Charles. "Today is your wedding day. Go. Be with your bride." Nodding his head, he swallowed. "She is a wonderful woman. You have, indeed, chosen well. I should never have doubted you."

"Thank you," Charles mumbled. Robert felt his brother's calculating eyes sweep over him as though he could see into his soul. Never had they lied to each other, always knowing deep down that no matter what if there was one person in the world who would understand, it would be the other.

"Fine," Charles said, rising to his feet. "I'll leave you to your own devices...for tonight." Leaning on the backrest of his chair, he lowered his head, eyes meeting his brother's, a hint of a challenge in them. "But tomorrow, you will tell me what is bothering you, do you understand? You will not leave here until I know what is going on!" His eyes narrowed. "And do not even think about sneaking away in the middle of the night!" He took a deep breath, his eyes betraying the anger he felt. "Robert, I swear, should you do so, I will hunt you to the end of the world. There is no place on this earth where I won't find you. Do you hear me?"

Looking up and meeting his brother's eyes, Robert smirked. "I love you, too, Brother."

"Are you scared?" From far away, Adriana's voice drifted to her ears.

Blinking, Isabella found herself staring at her own, rather pale reflection in the tall vanity mirror. Her sister stood behind her, brushing out her hair. "Where is Mother?" Isabella asked, glancing around the room.

"I asked her to leave because I wanted to talk to you," Adriana said, setting down the brush. Taking her sister's hand, she pulled her away from the vanity and next to her onto the settee. As their eyes met, Adriana frowned. "What is the matter? You seem different. Did you quarrel with Charles?"

"No," Isabella whispered, unable to meet her sister's eyes. How on earth was she to explain what had happened that day? She couldn't even understand it herself.

Never had she believed in love at first sight. No matter what her parents had told her about how they had met, deep down, Isabella had always thought that love developed over time. That day by day it

would grow until it shone through people's eyes. The idea of love at first sight had been nothing but a fairy tale to her. Something to inspire children to believe in the good in people. Something rakes used in order to seduce gullible, young women.

Was she a gullible, young woman? Were the feelings she was experiencing right now nothing but a short-lived infatuation? Would it pass within a matter of days?

Closing her eyes, Isabella shook her head.

"Isa, please," her sister whispered, cupping both hands around her sister's face. "You're scaring me."

Fighting the urge to let her tears spill freely down her cheeks, Isabella opened her eyes only to find her sister's looking into hers, concern clouding their usual sparkle. Isabella swallowed and then drew up the corners of her mouth and tried to smile at Adriana reassuringly. "It is nothing," she whispered. "I am just sad that from now on things will be different between us. We won't be able to see each other every day." A tear spilled over, and her sister brushed it away…just like Robert had not too long ago.

Shaking her head, Isabella pulled back, trying to focus her thoughts. "I'm sorry. I didn't mean to cry."

"Don't be sorry, Dear Sister," Adriana objected, her own eyes now shining with unspilled tears as well. "I will miss you, too." Shaking her head at herself, she sighed. "I didn't even realise it before. I was so busy trying to convince you that you were making a mistake in choosing Charles. However, now that you're actually married to him, I feel like my heart is breaking." Dabbing a handkerchief at her eyes, Adriana tried to smile. "I suppose my objections to you marrying Charles were never really based on him not being the right man for you but rather on him taking you away." New tears spilled forth. "I am sorry I tried to ruin this for you." A sob rose from her throat, and Isabella pulled her sister into her arms, smoothing back her hair.

"Don't be sorry," she whispered. "You didn't ruin anything. I do understand your motives, and I am glad you feel this way. You mean just as much to me, and I am very sorry that we'll have to part ways now." Pulling back, she looked into her sister's eyes. "But I promise that we'll see each other often. Maybe not every day but as often as we possibly can. Let's not be strangers, all right?"

Adriana nodded her head vigorously. "I promise."

5

A STOLEN HEART

After her sister left, Isabella felt exhausted. The emotional turmoil raging within her finally took its toll, and her eyelids began to grow heavy. Nevertheless, she couldn't just go to sleep and pretend nothing had happened. Her husband would soon come to her chamber and...

Taking a deep breath, Isabella stood by the window looking out at Bridgemoore's gardens. The night shrouded them in black, but the moon's silver light shone with such a magical force that it seemed like a million fairies were up and about, flitting in and out of the shadows.

Goosebumps rose on Isabella's arms, and she rubbed her hands over them, up and down, to chase them away, but it did not work. After all, it was not the cold that had brought them on but a trembling that rose from the depth of her being.

Shaking her head, Isabella wondered. Was she nervous about sharing a bed with her husband, whoever he was? Or would she be just as nervous if it was Robert she were waiting for?

Remembering how his dark eyes had looked into hers and had touched something deep within her, Isabella sighed. For a second, she closed her eyes, once more feeling the touch of his finger as it had skimmed away her tear. Goosebumps had risen on her arms then, too, and yet, she had not felt like this. She had not felt the desperate wish to get away and return to the life she had known before.

What was she to do?

There is nothing you can do, her voice of reason whispered. *You've made your choice.*

When the truth finally lay before her, Isabella broke down. Tears streaming down her face, she sank to the floor. Wrapping her arms around her knees, she rocked back and forth like she hadn't done since she had been a child. Hopelessness crushed her heart, and guilt invaded her soul.

Lost in her misery, she didn't hear the door opening. Neither did she hear her husband's footsteps as he rounded the bed and found his new bride weeping on the floor. Only when his strong arms picked her up, did she realise that he was there.

Too ashamed to look at him, she buried her face in his shirt and wept, unable to stop herself.

Not saying a word, Charles carried her to the bed and sat her down. Then he wrapped a blanket around her and pulled her back into his arms, holding her tight and whispering words of comfort.

For a long time, Isabella clung to him as if to a lifeboat saving her from the depths of the ocean. Her tears flowed freely, soaking his shirt as well as her nightgown. His arms never ceased their hold on her. Patiently, he rocked her, smoothing back her hair and whispering in her ear as though comforting an infant.

When her heart was finally cried out and her tears stopped, Isabella took a deep breath and tried to sit up.

Reluctantly, Charles released his hold on her. "Are you all right?"

Sighing, Isabella lifted her eyes to his, feeling the heat of embarrassment burn in her cheeks. "Thank you," was all she could say in that moment before her eyes dropped and her fingers busied themselves with the hem of her nightgown.

Leaning forward, he tried to look into her eyes. "Did I do something to upset you?"

As though slapped, Isabella's head shot up. "No! No, you didn't." Shaking her head, she stared at him, new tears threatening to spill forth. "Please, don't think that. It is not you." A shy smile came to her face. "You're wonderful. Truly wonderful."

He returned her smile. "If it is not me, can you tell me what happened? What has you so upset?"

Isabella drew in a sharp breath. She couldn't possibly tell him, could she? How would he react? What would he do?

Knowing that it didn't matter, Isabella sighed. This was her fault, not his. He deserved an explanation, some kind of explanation. At the very least, he deserved more than a weeping wife on his wedding night!

"I'm sorry, Charles," she began, trying to swallow the lump in her throat. "I never meant for this to happen. I never thought it could. I never…I never…"

Warm hands wrapped around hers, chasing away the chill that had them trembling. When she looked up, dark eyes so full of understanding and compassion looked into hers that Isabella almost lost control once again. How could she have done this to him?

"You're a wonderful man, Charles, and when I agreed to marry you, I thought we could be happy together," she began, not at all certain what to tell him.

He drew in a sharp breath, and the hands holding hers tensed. "What are you saying? You don't believe we can be happy together anymore?"

Closing her eyes, Isabella bit her lip. "I am such an awful person for doing this to you, but—"

"Doing what? What are you saying?" He dropped her hands, his voice apprehensive as he regarded her with suspicion in his eyes.

Focusing all the courage she could find, Isabella raised her gaze to his. "When I agreed to marry you, I believed with my heart and soul that this was what I wanted. I really did. I swear." She swallowed as a deeper understanding slowly began to cloud his eyes. "But then something happened. I…"

"Someone stole your heart," he whispered, closing his eyes, unable to look at her.

Shocked at his words, Isabella stared at him. "I'm so sorry. I didn't mean for it to happen."

His lips pressed into a thin line, and she could see the tension gripping his shoulders. His hands clenched and then unclenched before his eyes found hers once more. A sad smile flashed across his face then, and his head sank. "No one ever does."

"I'm so sorry, Charles. I don't know what to do. Maybe these feelings will go away. I hope they will. I don't want them. I…"

For a long moment, he looked into her eyes as though trying to read the truth in them. Then he sighed and shook his head. "After my mother died, my father never even considered remarrying. As children, Robert and I didn't understand why, but he always said that love was forever." A sad smile on his face, he nodded. "If you ever truly lose your heart to someone, you can never get it back. It is no longer yours, and whether or not that is wise does not matter. This is one choice we cannot make for ourselves. One choice that is made for us."

Hearing his words echo in her mind, Isabella realised how true they were. Deep down, she did not believe that her feelings were a mere infatuation. Deep down, she knew that she loved Robert; that she wanted him as her husband, not her brother-in-law.

Yet, here she was; in her bridal chamber sitting beside the man she had chosen to marry. Looking at him now, her heart broke all over again as she saw the sadness and disappointment clinging to his gentle features. All of his hopes had been dashed in one night. Just like hers.

"Why didn't you tell me?" Charles asked. "Before, I mean. I would not have held you to your promise."

Smiling at him through a curtain of tears, Isabella nodded. "I know. I just..." *I didn't know then*, she finished her thought, knowing she could never tell him. After everything she had done to him, she could not destroy the love he felt for his brother. No, she would never tell him who had stolen her heart minutes after she had given him her hand. Sighing, she shook her head. "What do we do now?"

"I don't know," Charles whispered, his eyes distant as though he didn't see her anymore. "I think I should go." He rose from the bed, a sad smile playing on his lips as he looked at her. "Get some sleep. You must be exhausted." Stepping back, he drew in a deep breath. "I need to think about..."

"I know," she whispered, watching him leave.

When the door finally closed behind him and she found herself alone again, her head sank down on her knees, and she closed her eyes. How differently this day had ended from how it had begun! What would tomorrow bring? How was she to act around her husband and her brother-in-law? Would Robert stay longer as he had suggested? Did she truly want him to?

Deep down, she knew that having Robert around would make everything more difficult; she would feel even more guilty whenever she saw him. And yet, she couldn't help but want him to stay. She wanted him near, to see him every day; to enjoy the feelings he had so unexpectedly awoken within her.

Isabella wanted all that, knowing it was wrong. Or at least her mind knew that it was. Her heart, however, refused to acknowledge it in any way. Her heart was selfish, unconcerned by the feelings of others, only seeking to be with the one person who made it shine.

Unfortunately, that person was Robert.

6

A FAVOUR ASKED

espite a massive headache tormenting him, Robert rose relatively early and found himself entering the breakfast parlour the moment his brother and Isabella prepared to exit. While Charles greeted him with an easy smile, Isabella could barely meet his eyes, a deep blush creeping up her cheeks.

Coming face to face with the nightmares that had kept him awake all night, Robert mumbled a greeting but otherwise kept his eyes on the floor and hastened over to his chair at the head of the table. He could almost feel his brother's eyes burning a hole into the back of his head.

"I will meet up with you as soon as I can," he heard Charles say before the door closed behind Isabella, and he heard her echoing footsteps retreating down the hall.

Robert took a deep breath, concentrating on the food before him. Instantly, a sickening feeling settled in his stomach that threatened to rise in his throat every time he dared lift the fork to his mouth. The usually intoxicating scents were beyond nauseating, and Robert pushed his plate away.

Swallowing, he raised his eyes, finding his brother's calculating gaze run over him like a blood hound sniffing out its prey. "What?"

Charles shrugged, waved away the footmen waiting by the door and settled into his usual seat, his eyes still intent on his brother. "You look awful," he finally said. "However, I suppose that was to be expected, and I dare not even hope this will be a lesson to you." He drew in a deep breath, leaning forward. "Tell me what brought on this rather childish behaviour."

Annoyed with his brother's parental attitude, Robert shook his head at him, instantly regretting this action though as a mind-splitting pain shot through his head. Groaning, he closed his eyes. "I merely enjoyed your wedding festivities. I doubt that is reason for concern."

"It would not be reason for concern if I believed you," Charles objected. "However, you do seem to forget that I know you, Brother. Maybe even better than you know yourself, and despite your two-year absence, I am confident that I am right about this." He took a deep breath then reached out a hand and placed it on Robert's arm. "You were different when you arrived here two days ago. Please, do not pretend that nothing happened for I know it to be a lie. And although I believe you capable of dealing with life in general, you seem shaken to the core in a way that has me greatly concerned. Talk to me, Brother. Who did this to you? What did this to you?"

Looking into his brother's eyes so full of honest concern and brotherly love, Robert felt his insides twist. More than anything, he wanted to confide in him, but he knew he could not.

Swallowing the lump in his throat, Robert tried to smile. "I appreciate your concern, but you are mistaken. I am perfectly fine." He grinned. "Well, maybe not perfectly fine. This headache might actually be the death of me."

Not in the least tempted to smile, Charles sat back, disappointment clouding his eyes. "What has changed, Robert? Why can you not confide in me anymore? Have I given you any reason to believe that you cannot trust me?"

Sighing, Robert closed his eyes. "Please let this go, Charles. I know you mean well, and believe me, there is no one in the world I trust more than you. But this," he took a deep breath, "this is something…you cannot know."

"I see." Still looking at him, Charles' eyes narrowed. "Then answer me this; have you done something unlawful?"

"What?" Robert gaped at him, unable to believe his ears. "Of course not. What makes you say this?"

Again, Charles leaned forward, and the left corner of his mouth drew up into a knowing grin. "Then I suppose it has to be a matter of the heart."

Robert swallowed.

"Not many things in this world have the power to shake a man to his core, and while I cannot speak from experience, I have witnessed the effects of a woman on a man's heart here and there. The good and the bad." He smiled. "Was she at the wedding? Does she not return your affections?"

Again, Robert swallowed. "No, she…I mean…" Hesitating for but a moment, he met his brother's eyes. "She was, yes, and you're right. She does not care for me. There, are you satisfied?"

Charles shook his head. "Do not lie to me, Robert. I am not this easily fooled. I can tell that you simply wish for me to refrain from questioning you further." He rose from his chair. "I apologise for intruding into your life, but as your brother, I'm afraid I cannot help it." He shrugged, and a sad smile came to his face. "Maybe I am being selfish, for my happiness could never be complete without yours." He took a deep breath. "Be that as it may, I'm afraid I need to be off. Before you came in, I was just informed of a quarrel between tenants that seems to be getting out of hand."

Surprised, Robert asked, "What about Mr. Hill? Is that not usually a steward's job?"

"It is," Charles confirmed. "However, his wife went into labour last night so I cannot call upon him. His mind is elsewhere as it needs to be." Nodding at him, Charles turned and walked to the door. However, before he left, he looked back at his brother. "I cannot say how long I will be occupied today. Could I ask a favour?"

"Of course."

"If your current state allows for it, would you show Isabella around the estate?" Robert's heart skipped a beat. "I do not wish for her to feel neglected today; after all we've been only married for a day." An apologetic smile crossed over his face.

"I will," Robert said, knowing deep in his heart that he should have refused. However, as much as he knew what he ought to do, he could not. At the thought of seeing Isabella, his heart jumped with joy, and all the nerve endings in his body began to tingle with anticipation.

"Thank you," Charles said and left.

Burying his face in his hands, Robert closed his eyes, praying for the strength to keep his hands off his brother's wife.

7

NOTORIOUS NORWOOD

After searching almost the entire house, Robert finally stumbled upon Isabella in the small back parlour, that—as it faced north—usually saw few visitors. "I am sorry to intrude," he said upon opening the door.

Startled, she lifted her eyes off the closed book in her hands, and her cheeks glowed a slight pink. "No, not at all," she objected, shaking her head.

Closing the door, Robert did not know what to do. Should he sit down beside her? Or rather in the armchair across from her? Or should he remain standing?

You should leave, his voice of reason whispered. Taking a deep breath, Robert ignored it. "I thought I'd find you with your sister and your parents."

Her eyes shifting between him and the window, she shrugged and laid down the book beside her. "They went for a ride."

"And you did not join them?"

"I told them I would spend the day with Charles."

Robert frowned. "But he was called away."

"I know," she whispered, her eyes meeting his for but a second. "I wanted to be alone." Taking a deep breath, she rose from the settee and went to stand by the window. "It is a beautiful day, is it not?"

"I suppose it is." Sadness clung to her like a blanket, and Robert felt the desperate need to hold her, wrap her in his arms and never let go. Instead, he asked, "Is there anything I can do?"

She turned to look at him then. "That is very kind of you, but I believe my husband will return shortly."

Nodding, Robert gritted his teeth. "I suppose he will." He swallowed. "Allow me to take this opportunity, my lady, to wish you…and my brother a happy marriage." As the blood began to boil in his veins, Robert's hands balled into fists.

"I believe you've already done so," she reminded him, her dark eyes drilling into his as though she could read his mind. "It makes me wonder if you truly mean what you say."

Robert felt himself shake with the effort it took to keep himself under control. "Why would you doubt my words? Do you not believe I wish my brother to be happy?"

"I do believe so, yes," she said, her eyes closing for a second. Then she shook her head, and a single tear rolled down her cheek. "As do I. He is a good man, and he truly deserves to be happy. I only fear that…"

His heart hammering in his chest, Robert stepped forward, his feet carrying him to her side of their own accord. "What do you fear, my lady?"

She sighed, brushing the wetness from her cheek, then met his eyes. "I fear I will not be the means to ensure that."

"What makes you say this?" he whispered. Mesmerised by the slight quiver in her lips, Robert felt himself lean closer. His eyes travelled over her face, seeing her shiver as his breath brushed over her cheek.

"Do you truly have to ask?" she whispered and lifted her eyes to meet his. Open and without a hint of embarrassment, she looked at him, seemingly hoping against hope that he might know the answer to their troubles, that somehow he would know what to do.

Robert sighed for he knew that there was nothing that could be done. The moment she had whispered her 'I do', she had not only become his brother's wife but also, as far as the law was concerned, Robert's sister.

If only he had a brother's love for her.

As he stood so close to her, Isabella breathed in his scent and for a second closed her eyes. In a way, it reminded her of Charles, and yet, it was completely different, new and unknown. It spoke of a different man; one she did not know yet, but desperately wished she would.

Meeting his eyes, she sighed, feeling her limbs begin to tremble as his gaze slid over her in an all too familiar way—completely inappropriate for a brother-in-law, though. However, she could not bring herself to tell him so.

Instead, she smiled, enjoying the tingle that went over her as she did. "I have heard of you, Lord Norwood," she whispered, watching his eyes narrow as she spoke. "The notorious Viscount known for his…adventures all over London."

He drew in a deep breath, looking displeased with the direction their conversation had taken. And yet, the hint of an amused smile drew up the corners of his mouth. "Adventures, you say. Would you care to elaborate?"

Feeling the hint of a blush warm her cheeks, Isabella averted her eyes, but only for a moment. Surprised to find herself so daring, she could not keep herself from teasing him further—to his obvious delight. "My lord, I would not dare. Adventures like yours are not meant for a lady's ears."

A deep smile came to his face then, and his eyes began to sparkle as he took yet another step closer. Isabella felt her heart almost jump out of her chest as he leaned down and whispered, "My lady, how would you know if you've never even heard them yourself? Are you suggesting that you are not a lady?"

Isabella's eyes widened in feigned shock, and she gasped at his insinuation. "I would never dare suggest such a thing, my lord. I was merely informed that stories unfit for a lady's ears are the reason for your reputation. However, I never heard them myself." Except for snippets overheard here and there, Isabella thought, shocked at her own boldness to confront him in such a way. "I was advised to keep my distance from you, my lord."

"Is that so?" he asked, his eyes travelling down to her lips. "And why is that? Do you fear for your reputation?"

Isabella swallowed, and for a second, her gaze travelled down to his mouth before meeting his eyes once more. "Should I?" she whispered, and the teasing smile vanished from his face.

He drew in a deep breath, all signs of amusement gone replaced by a serious tone that she had never seen on him before.

How could you? Her voice of reason whispered. *You hardly know him.*

"No," he finally said, his lips pressing into a thin line. She could see the tension in his jaw as he swallowed and then took a step backward. "You have nothing to fear from me, my lady."

A shy smile came to Isabella's face as her heart rejoiced, and, yet, felt a pang of regret at the same time. Despite all the rumours she had heard, Lord Norwood seemed to be an honourable man. He had wanted to kiss her; she had seen it in his eyes, but he hadn't.

However, a part of her could not help but feel disappointed. Never before had she felt the deep desire to have a man's lips caress her own. Why did he have to be so blasted honourable?

At the thought, a deep blush came to Isabella's cheeks, and she turned her head away. How could she think such things? Married but a day, and to his brother no less. Was she the most awful creature to ever walk the earth?

Guilt washed over her like a downpour, and she closed her eyes. Why did this have to happen? Everything had been so perfect. Charles was her match. Her perfect match. They suited each other in every way.

Every way?

"Are you all right?"

Lifting her eyes to his, Isabella shook her head. "I hardly know."

Deep down, something had awakened. Something that sent a shiver down her back every time this man looked at her. Something that made her want to reach out and wrap her arms around him. Something that urged her to forget the vows she had made.

"You look pale, my lady." His voice was but a whisper, and still, it shook her to her very core. "Are you feeling unwell?"

"Unwell?" she echoed as though to herself. "Indeed." Shaking her head, a sad smile drew up the corners of her mouth. "I suppose I must be. No woman ought to think such things, feel such…" Closing her eyes, she took a deep breath. When she opened them again, his face

was but a breath's length away from hers, tortured eyes looking into her soul.

Isabella drew in a sharp breath.

"You feel it too, do you not?" he whispered as his arm came around her, holding her close. "At first, I thought I was imagining it, but then…" He gritted his teeth, a look of pure agony darkening his eyes. Taking a deep breath, he hung his head. Slowly, ever so slowly, it sank until his forehead came to rest against hers. "Part of me wishes I had never returned," he whispered, and she felt the breath of his words against her lips. "I was fine," he continued, then lifted his head and looked into her eyes. "I was fine before I met you."

A sad smile came to Isabella's face. "So was I." She swallowed, acutely aware of his arms around her as well as her own body's reaction to his closeness. "What are we to do?"

A look of madness came to his eyes, and he shook his head. "I have not the faintest idea," he said, raking his left hand through his hair. "All I know is that you're…," he took a deep breath, "you're my brother's wife." His jaw clenched as he looked at her. "But every time I see you, I just…" He stopped and inhaled deeply, his eyes travelling down to her lips. "I want to do things I shouldn't even be thinking."

Feeling herself tremble, Isabella nodded. "Me too."

His eyes opened wide, and he searched her face. "Truly?"

Once more, Isabella nodded, knowing that if she should speak again, her voice would be choked by tears. Pressing her lips together, she forced them back.

"If you were anyone else's wife," he whispered, his arm tightening around her possessively, "I would not hesitate." He shook his head, his eyes burning into hers. "I would whisk you away to the end of the world if need be. Nothing would…" Stopping, he closed his eyes.

When he looked at her again, all the fire she had seen in them before was gone. "But you're not," he whispered, resignation ringing in his voice. "You're my brother's wife, and no amount of wishful thinking is going to change that." He released her then and took a step back.

Isabella felt the loss of his closeness like an icy draft, and a shiver ran down her back. Instantly, her arms came up to reach for him, but felt nothing except cold air. Balling her hands into fists, she forced them back down to her sides. "I do not wish to hurt him, either," she finally said, swallowing as a sob threatened to escape her throat.

Nodding, he barely looked at her. "I should leave," he mumbled, then spun around and strode from the room.

Staring after him, Isabella wondered if she had only imagined him, so inexplicably fast had he entered her life and left it the same way. Allowing her tears to flow freely, she sank down on the settee and wept.

8

THE WRONG SISTER

obert was certain that before the day was out, he would lose his mind.

While reason advised him to keep a safe distance from his brother's wife, fate continued to throw them together.

Leaving her in the parlour after their close encounter, Robert tried his utmost to keep himself busy. His thoughts, however, refused to linger anywhere else but on Isabella's beautiful face. When dinner was served and his brother still hadn't returned, Robert found himself seated at the long table in the dining room, Isabella and Adriana to his right and the earl and his wife to his left. For all intents and purposes, he was surrounded.

Taking a deep breath, he forced his eyes onto his plate and busied himself cutting his food into even slices. He should never have returned home!

Whenever the earl or his wife addressed him, Robert would look up, forcing his eyes to ignore the vision sitting a mere arm's length to his right. However, occasionally his determination would fail him, and he would steal a glance at his brother's wife.

Her head bowed, eyes focused on her food, Isabella looked nothing like the radiant bride she should have been. Misery clung to her like a thick fog, and Robert couldn't help but wonder why no one else noticed.

Happily chatting about their ride through the meadows bordering Bridgemoore to the north, Adriana seemed oblivious to her sister's silent pain. Her eyes glowed, and she beamed at Robert in a way that he had not noticed before.

Possibly because his attention had been focused on her sister, instead.

As he looked at her now, he finally realised what was going on.

Adriana was trying to catch his eye.

Recounting their ride that morning, she solely seemed to address Robert, not her sister. Her eyes were focused on his, and she would occasionally avert them in a seemingly shy, yet calculated manner, only to raise them again a moment later, a dazzling smile on her face.

Robert took a deep breath. Why couldn't he have fallen for Adriana?

Just like Isabella, she had her mother's dark, exotic features. Her smiles, while calculated, seemed genuine and spoke of a kind heart. She was lively and attentive. Most importantly, however, she was available.

Could he come to care for her? Robert wondered. In so many ways, they were so much alike. And yet, when he looked into Adriana's sparkling eyes, none of the overwhelming emotions flooded his heart that had swept him off his feet the moment he had seen Isabella. How could that be? He hardly knew either one of them. Why did Adriana not stir the same feelings in his heart that Isabella did?

As a war waged within himself, Robert hardly noticed how dinner passed. Did he eat at all? He could not be sure.

As soon as they rose from their seats, Adriana suggested they gather in the front parlour where the pianoforte stood. "I've brought some new sheet music," she said, smiling up at him. "But you must promise that you will give your honest opinion, my lord."

Robert nodded, forcing the corners of his mouth into a smile. "I certainly shall."

Catching Isabella's eye, he thought to detect a hint of displeasure before she focused her gaze back onto the floor.

Robert gritted his teeth, knowing only too well the surge of jealous rage that had almost overtaken him at the thought of her sharing his brother's bed. Pushing the thought from his mind lest he do something he would regret later, he joined his guests in the parlour.

A delighted smile on her lips, Adriana looked at him, then took her seat behind the pianoforte and began to play.

Her fingers flew over the keys with grace, revealing her to be a refined musician. Clearly, her performance was meant to impress him as she frequently lifted her eyes off the *new* sheet music to look at him.

Forcing a smile on his face whenever she did was all he could do. His attention, however, was directed at the woman sitting beside him. Acutely aware of her scent, her slightly elevated breathing as well as the warmth radiating from her body, Robert swallowed, his hands balling into fists.

The second Adriana finished her first piece, Robert jumped to his feet. Assuring her in the most flourishing words what a talented musician she was, he quickly excused himself, stating that unexpected business needed his immediate attention.

Though disappointed, no one objected, and with a final bow, Robert almost ran from the room.

Once he reached the hall, he took a deep breath, feeling relief wash over him. Nevertheless, he dreaded every step that took him farther away from Isabella. What had she done to him? He shook his head, blindly running through the house, desperate for a place where he could calm his nerves.

Without attention to his surroundings, Robert was surprised when he once again found himself near the small back parlour. Sighing, he entered the room.

Staring at the window overlooking a corner of the rose garden, Robert could almost imagine Isabella standing beside him. He took a step forward and closed his eyes, leaning his forehead against the cool window pane. What was he to do?

Lifting his head, he crossed his arms, feeling his body tense as his mind and heart battled for supremacy. He knew what he wanted; what he could never have.

A desperate rage surged within him at the situation he found himself in, and before he knew it, an agonising groan rose from his lips. Of its own accord, his right arm pulled back, and his fist collided with the wall.

A blinding pain shot through his arm. Still, it was the sharp intake of air coming from the door that caught his attention and made him spin around.

Standing in the door frame was Isabella, a shocked expression on her beautiful face. "My lord, what are you doing?" she gasped, her eyes travelling back and forth between his face and his curled hand. Stepping toward him, she reached out her own, then seemed to think better of it and pulled it back. "I...is your hand hurt?"

Taking a deep breath, Robert couldn't help the angry snort that escaped his lips. "It is not my hand that is hurt, my lady."

At his words, she dropped her eyes to the floor, but not before he had seen a glimpse of understanding in them. "What are you doing here?" he whispered, trying to distract his thoughts from the intoxicating scent that threatened to cloud his mind. "I had thought you were with your family."

"I was," she answered, lifting her eyes to his. "But I couldn't...I...I didn't want to lie to them. I don't want to pretend to be happy when I am not." She shook her head as though unable to believe her own words. "But neither do I want them to know the truth." Sighing, she stepped around him. "I thought I'd come here and read," she said, picking up the book she had left on the settee earlier that morning. "I didn't think you'd be here."

Robert shrugged, absentmindedly stretching his fingers, enjoying the pain, hoping it somehow would offset the pain in his heart. "My feet led me here." He closed his eyes for but a moment, and the dam broke. "I can't stop thinking about you."

Her eyes widened, and she swallowed. "You must not say such things, my lord," she whispered, shaking her head. "It is not right."

"I know," he hissed, gritting his teeth. "After all, he is *my* brother." As the pain spread into every fibre of his being, he stepped toward her, unable to hold himself back.

Again, she drew in a sharp breath, but her eyes shifted upward, finding his.

As his heart hammered in his chest, Robert reached out and cupped his hand to her face. Feeling the softness of her skin brush against his, his other arm came around her waist, pulling her closer.

All the while, Isabella stood as though frozen; however, she did not resist. Transfixed, her eyes gazed into his, and he could see the same struggle on her face that he felt in his heart. Her breath came in

short gasps, and when his head slowly dipped lower, her eyes travelled to his lips.

As temptation urged him on, Robert's insides twisted into knots. Knowing the betrayal he was committing, his mind screamed at him to stop, and yet, his heart only saw the love shining in Isabella's eyes. How could he not?

A breath away from her lips, he stopped and swallowed. Closing his eyes, he rested his forehead against hers. As a shiver ran through her, he lifted his head. "I'm sorry. I shouldn't have." He took a step back, releasing his hold on her.

When his hand left her face, a sob escaped her lips, and she grasped his hand, looking up into his eyes. "Neither should I," Isabella whispered, her fingers caressing the palm of his hand.

Almost holding his breath, Robert glanced down at their linked hands, and another surge of desire swept through him.

"There you are," Charles spoke out from behind him.

Isabella flinched, and her eyes went wide, staring into his.

Instantly, Robert dropped her hand and took a step back. Forcing a smile on his face, he turned to meet his brother's eyes. "I see, you have returned. Is everything settled then?" As his pulse hammered in his veins, Robert stared at Charles, wondering if his brother suspected anything. How long had he been standing in the door?

"It is, yes," Charles said, watchful eyes travelling from his brother to his wife.

Isabella stepped forward, a strained smile on her face. "I am pleased to hear that."

For a second, Robert feared that all was lost, but then Charles held out his hand to his wife and once she'd taken it drew her arm through his. His hand cupping hers, he smiled at her. "I apologise for leaving you alone today."

Seeing his brother's hands on the woman he loved, Robert felt his muscles tense. Involuntarily, his hands balled into fists, and he had to grit his teeth to force down an agonising groan that threatened to rise from his throat. After all, his brother had every right to touch her; she was his wife.

Then Charles turned to him, brotherly affection shining in his eyes, and a new wave of guilt washed over Robert as though the skies had opened and soaked him through. "Thank you for keeping her company, Robert. I appreciate it."

"You're welcome," he forced out, his jaw clenched. "It was my pleasure."

"I trust he has made you feel welcome," Charles asked his new bride, affection and warmth ringing in his voice.

Averting her eyes for but a second, Isabella tried to smile at her husband. "He has."

"Good," Charles said. "After all, we're family now."

As though someone had stabbed him in the heart, Robert felt a searing pain run through his body. Excusing himself, he hastened out of the room, ran down the corridor and left the house.

Saddling a random horse, he chased the sky across the meadows north of Bridgemoore. As the wind swept over his face, pulling on his hair, tears ran from his eyes, and for a split second, he thought to end it all, then and there.

After all, he was already in hell; what did he have to lose?

9

UNREQUITED LOVE

"Robert is a bit of a hot-head at times," Charles explained as they strolled through the gardens, "but he has a good heart. Do not allow his rather rugged attire to fool you into believing him a lesser man."

Drawing a deep breath, Isabella shook her head. "Of course not. After all, he is your brother, and I trust that you know him best."

Stopping, Charles turned to her. A smile on his face, he gazed into her eyes. "Have I ever told you how beautiful you are?" he whispered, and Isabella's stomach turned into knots. "I don't believe I have." He shook his head to clear it. "Well, then I'll do it now." Cupping his hands to her face, he looked at her with such deep devotion that Isabella felt her knees begin to shake. "I never noticed until this day—now that you're my wife—how truly amazing you are. You shine, inside and out, and to be in your presence makes me feel alive like I have never felt before."

Isabella swallowed, temporarily forgetting to smile. Not having expected such an affectionate speech, she felt a slight tingle run through her at his words. He truly was a wonderful man, and in that moment, Isabella knew that she could have loved him.

If it hadn't been for Robert.

The slight tingle she felt at Charles' profession of affection was nothing compared to the searing fire a mere look from Robert could set ablaze within her.

You're married to the wrong brother, her mind whispered, and Isabella wanted to slap herself for having been so careless with regard to her heart's desire. If she had only heeded her sister's advice.

If only.

Closing her eyes for a moment, Isabella forced her attention back to the man before her. "Thank you," she whispered. "Thank you for those beautiful words."

A smile lifted the corners of his mouth. "You're most welcome."

Isabella took a deep breath. "However, I have to say that they surprise me."

"They do?"

Isabella nodded. "Yes, especially after…my confession last night." Averting her eyes, she looked out over the grassy plains before her. "Are you not angry with me? I thought you would be. What husband would not if his wife told him what I told you?"

When he remained silent, she lifted her eyes off the ground.

Neither anger nor disappointment showed on his face, and he drew her hands into his, smiling encouragingly. "When you accepted my proposal, neither one of us spoke of great love, did we?" Isabella shook her head. "You never promised me your heart, and now I have no right to complain."

Isabella stared at him.

"Do not misunderstand me," Charles continued. "I have no intention of seeing either one of us suffer in this marriage because of an unrequited love." He smiled, brushing a strand of her dark tresses behind her ear. "Trust in me, Isabella, and I will show you that sometimes dreams do come true."

A silent tear rolled down her cheek as she stared at the man she had married. She had never known that he held so much love and devotion in his heart. If only she could love him back!

"Let's speak of this no more," Charles interrupted her thoughts. "At least, not while your family is still here. And my brother." Isabella felt a small stab in her heart at his reminder. "But before long, your family will return home and my brother will go...wherever the road leads him, and then we will have time to find our own way. All right?"

"All right." Isabella nodded, feeling a lump settle in her throat at the thought of saying goodbye to Robert. And yet, there was no other way!

Strolling down the path toward the small pavilion in the rose garden, Isabella fought a rising panic at the thought of what awaited her down the road. What would her life be like, now that all of her priorities had shifted so unexpectedly?

As they walked around the corner to the small pavilion, to their surprise, they found it already occupied. "Adriana? What are you doing here?" Isabella asked. "I thought you were playing your music."

The hint of a pout on her face, she sighed. "Well, I suppose I must play quite poorly considering that Lord Norwood as well as yourself almost fled the room."

Stumped, Isabella began to stutter, acutely aware of her husband's presence. "Well, I...You know, I simply..."

"This sounds like something personal among sisters," Charles said smiling. "I'll see you at supper." He gave her a kiss on the forehead and then walked away.

Sitting down next to her sister, Isabella took a deep breath. "I apologise. I never meant to insult your playing in any way. It's just..."

"You wanted to spend some time with your husband," Adriana finished for her, a forgiving smile on her face. "Don't worry. I understand. I was never truly angry with you. I suppose I was more disappointed that Lord Norwood...or Robert...do you think I can call him Robert? After all, we're family now."

"I suppose," Isabella said, knowing exactly what Adriana was trying to say. All throughout dinner, she had observed her sister's excitement whenever Robert had looked her way. She had seen the sparkle that had lit up her eyes and the charming smile she had used to draw his attention. It had taken all of Isabella's willpower to remain in her seat, seemingly oblivious to what was playing out right before her eyes. "Do you care for him?" she asked, feeling the tension in her heart spread throughout her body.

Adriana grinned, and a slight blush coloured her cheeks. "He is quite dashing, wouldn't you say?"

"I suppose so."

"You do not mind, do you?" Adriana asked, narrowed eyes searching Isabella's face.

Isabella swallowed, trying to smile. "Of course, not. Why would I?"

Adriana shrugged then shook her head. Once again, her face began to glow. "Imagine! If I were to marry him, then we could all live here together! Wouldn't that be wonderful?" She laughed. "Two sisters married to two brothers. Fate plays a strange game sometimes, doesn't it?"

"I suppose so," was all Isabella could manage. The idea of her sister marrying Robert turned her stomach upside down. The thought, however, of them all living under the same roof was torture. Forced to see the man that she loved with her own sister day in and day out would surely drive her mad.

It sounded like her worst nightmare, and yet, Isabella couldn't help but wonder if her sister's hopes were justified. If Robert could not have her, would he ever consider marrying Adriana?

Brushing down his horse, Robert tried to clear his head.

"What am I to do?" he whispered to the brown mare, who continued to munch her oats, ignoring him completely.

Getting away from the manor, Robert had revelled in the race across the fields, feeling the wind in his face as though it could sweep away his troubled thoughts. His hair was a tangled mess, and his cheeks glowed with the chill that still clung to the air.

Although the thought to leave, to keep riding and not return, had been more than tempting, he knew he could not take the coward's way out. His brother deserved more, and so did Isabella.

The door to the stables swung open, and a beam of light lit up the cobblestone path leading down to the box where Robert tended to his horse. Footsteps approached, and without turning his head, Robert knew who had come to pay him a visit.

"There you are," his brother's voice rang out behind him. "A part of me thought you would not return." Stepping into the box, Charles came to stand on the other side of the mare. "Why will you not talk to me, Robert?"

Robert shrugged, keeping his eyes fixed on the mare's coat. "Because there is nothing to talk about."

"I thought we had already established that there was," Charles objected. "I thought I'd asked you not to lie to me."

"Fine!" Robert snapped, tossing the brush into the box by his feet. "Then let's just say I don't want to talk about it. Why can you not accept that? Believe me, you're better off not knowing." Biting his tongue, Robert stalked out of the box before he could say something he would regret later.

Unfortunately, Charles could not be discouraged that easily. "I cannot accept it," he said, coming after him, "because it pains you. I can see it on your face. Let me help! Please! Tell me, and I promise you'll feel better."

Robert spun around, staring at his brother, and for a moment, he actually believed his words to be true. He had never kept a secret from his brother and doing so now felt more than just wrong. It almost felt like a betrayal in itself. And yet, an inner voice whispered in his ear, warning him that sharing this particular secret would only do harm. How could it not?

"Please," Charles repeated. Stepping toward him, he placed his hands on Robert's shoulders, his eyes intent on his brother's. "Let me help."

Closing his eyes, Robert shook his head. "I can't." Seeing the concern on his brother's face, he shrugged. "I'm sorry, but I can't. I know you mean well, but this is something I have to deal with on my own. I cannot involve you. It wouldn't be fair."

"I'm your brother," Charles insisted. "There is nothing I wouldn't do for you."

An iron fist closed around Robert's heart, squeezing the life from him. "I know." He swallowed. "And for that very reason, I cannot tell you."

Frowning, Charles looked him up and down, searching for the answer Robert wouldn't give. "All right," he finally said. "But know I am here whenever you need me."

"Thank you, Brother."

Charles took a deep breath. "Then let me ask you something else?"

Robert nodded, wondering what else his brother could possibly want to know.

"What do you think of Isabella now that you have spent some time with her?"

Taken aback, Robert's eyes widened, and a shiver went down his back. "She's...she's a wonderful woman," he stammered.

"Do you truly think so?" Charles asked. "You are my brother, and it is my dearest wish that you like her. After all, we are family now." He smiled. "And maybe, just maybe, your way will lead you home more often now. I've missed you, Robert."

Torn between love and guilt, Robert stared at his brother until a belated smile slowly tucked up the corners of his mouth. "I've missed you, too," he said, knowing it to be true. And yet, he knew that once he left Bridgemoore again, he would probably not return.

How could he?

10

UNBEARABLE TEMPTATION

Standing by the window in the front drawing room, Robert stared out into the rain. Heavy drops pelted the ground, forming fast puddles here and there. Dark clouds hung in the sky, blocking out the sun and promising even more rain.

Robert leaned his head against the cool window pane and sighed, hoping against hope that his gloomy thoughts were only an echo of the forces raging outside. If only they would disappear as easily as the dark clouds hanging in the sky.

For the past hour, he had thought about his brother's words and come to no other conclusion but to leave Bridgemoore for good. He loved Isabella, and he could not bear the thought of watching her be his brother's wife. And yet, he loved Charles just as much. If it had been any other man, he would simply have stolen her away in the middle of the night, but he could not betray Charles.

Robert knew he had a duty to Bridgemoore, but he had never cared about the title and felt certain his brother would do far better than he ever could in managing the estate's business. After all, he had done so all these years!

From down the hall, footsteps echoed as they approached. Then Charles' voice cut through the silence. "Where is Robert? Go and find him!"

Hearing the edge in his brother's voice, Robert opened the door. "What is going on?" As he looked from Charles to Adriana, Robert felt his heart speed up. Both their faces held the same worry edged into their eyes, their jaws clenched.

"Isabella went for a walk, and she has not returned," his brother explained.

"What?" Robert stared out the window into the pouring rain. "How long has she been gone?"

Adriana shrugged, her cheeks pale with fear. "I'm not sure. We were outside in the rose garden, and she said she wanted to take a stroll to clear her mind." Her eyes were almost pleading as they looked at him. "She said she wouldn't be long. She said she'd be back before supper."

"That was half an hour ago," Charles added, and Robert realised that he had forgotten about supper altogether. "I am worried, Robert. I have to go find her."

"I'll help you." Grabbing his coat, he hurried for the door.

Charles followed close behind him. "I was hoping you'd say that."

"Do you know which direction she went?" Robert called over his shoulder as he pulled open the door and the drumming rain almost drowned out his voice.

"North," Adriana stammered, staring into the downpour. "I think she headed north."

By the time the brothers reached the stables, they were soaked through. Not waiting for the stable boys, they quickly saddled their horses, feeling the need to hurry in their trembling limbs.

Pulling himself into the saddle, Charles looked over to his brother. "I'll go north-east, you'll go north-west. We'll meet in the middle."

Robert had barely time to nod before Charles' gelding shot past him into the rain and was lost from sight a moment later.

Urging on his mare, Robert followed, turning north-east. As the rain drummed down on his scalp and shoulders, fear crept into his heart. What if they didn't find her? Where had she gone?

In the half-dark, the world looked different, especially through the curtain of rain that hung before his eyes. Constantly afraid, he might overlook her, Robert slowed his horse. Squinting his eyes, he peered out into the rain, trying to catch a glimpse of his surroundings. When had it started to rain? Where had she been then? Probably too far from the manor or she would have returned, he thought. Where else could she have sought shelter?

Nothing but wet grass stretched before his feet. Craning his neck, he spotted the small chestnut grove where they had often played as children. Almost hidden in the dark, its tall trees stood like a green wall side by side in a half-circle.

Urging his mare on, Robert leaned forward, once again squinting his eyes against the rain.

At first, he could spot nothing but tall trunks and densely growing treetops. But as he drew nearer, he saw something move close to a tree stem on the eastern side of the grove. Directing his horse toward it, he held his breath.

Then he saw her, and relief flooded his heart.

Crouched on the ground, Isabella had her arms wrapped around her knees, her clothes and hair dripping wet and clinging to her skin.

When he approached, she looked up and then rose to her feet, her eyes locked on his face.

"Are you all right?" he called through the deafening drum of the downpour.

She nodded her head as he pulled up his reins and jumped to the ground. Dropping the reins, he strode toward her, holding out his hands to her

However, seeing his intention, Isabella took a step back, shaking her head.

Frowning, Robert stopped. "Are you all right?"

"You should leave," Isabella said, wrapping her arms around her middle as her limbs began to tremble. Tears rolled down her face, and for a moment, she closed her eyes. "Why did you come?" she sobbed.

"How could I not?" Robert asked dumbfounded and took a careful step closer. "Why did you walk this far from the manor? Let me take you home."

Isabella shook her head, despair clinging to her eyes. "I…I didn't notice. I just walked. I wanted to get away—if only for a moment." Her voice broke. "I don't know what to do. Please, tell me what to do."

Hanging his head, Robert sighed. "I can't for I am just as lost."

"Are you?" she asked, and her eyes narrowed. Then she lifted her head. "Will you marry Adriana?"

"What?" Robert's eyes went wide as though she had just punched him in the stomach. "Why would you ask that?"

"She is my sister," Isabella said, her hands closing more tightly around her arms. "In many ways, she is just like me, and she cares for you." Lifting her eyes to his, she stepped forward. "You cannot have me, but you can have her."

As the breath caught in his throat, Robert's eyes narrowed. "She may be your sister, but she is not you," he snapped, stepping closer. "Do you truly think so little of me that you just assume I do not care which sister I bed?"

Although he could see that she had to force herself not to avert her eyes, a deep blush crept up her cheeks. "I didn't mean it like that," she whispered, and he had to strain his ear to hear her.

Robert snorted as the blood pulsed in his veins. "Considering your suggestion, you should have no problem being my brother's wife." He lowered his head, his eyes drilling into hers. "After all, he is just like me."

Isabella drew in a sharp breath. "He is not," she said. "I'm sorry. I shouldn't have said that. I just...I don't know what to do."

Straightening, Robert inhaled deeply. "I will leave Bridgemoore come morning." Isabella's eyes widened. "Then I will be out of your way, and you can...you can...," he trailed off, unable to finish even the thought of what good his departure might mean for his brother's marriage.

"I don't want you to leave," she finally said, sadness clinging to her eyes, making him almost retract his words. "However, I know that you have to. It's inevitable and probably for the best. But...before you go, there is something I would ask of you?"

"What is it?"

She swallowed and met his eyes. "Would you kiss me?"

Robert's eyes went wide as he tried to make sense of her words.

"Just once," she added. "I just...I want to know what it feels like."

All of a sudden, anger surged through his body, and his hands balled into fists. "Why?" he snorted. "So that you can compare my kiss to my brother's?"

Startled by his sudden outburst, Isabella took a step back. For a long time, her eyes stared into his before she shook her head. "He never touched me."

Robert's eyes narrowed. "Never?"

"Never." Taking a deep breath, she stepped toward him, her hands coming to rest on the front of his shirt. Lifting her head, she looked at him, her eyes almost pleading.

His chest rose and fell beneath her fingertips, and Isabella could feel the warmth of his skin through the wet layer of clothing separating them. Looking into his eyes, she saw the struggle he faced as the muscles in his jaw clenched.

"Just once," she whispered, selfishly hoping that the temptation was too great for him to resist. Even though her mind knew her request to be morally wrong, her heart could not bear the thought of never knowing his touch.

Slowly, ever so slowly, his hands came around her waist as though he had to fight himself every step of the way.

Feeling his arms pull her closer against his body, Isabella rejoiced, enjoying the unexpected tingles that ran through her being.

His gaze searched her face, now and again lowering from her eyes to her lips. Breathing hard, he whispered, "Just once," as though to convince himself that once was not the transgression he knew it to be.

When his lips finally brushed against hers, Isabella's knees went weak, and she sagged against him.

Instantly, his arms closed around her, holding her upright and pressing her into his body. She moaned, and her arms wrapped around his neck.

Feeling her respond, he deepened the kiss, his mouth tasting every curve of her lips, her mouth, her tongue. Once awakened, his hunger knew no bounds. His hands travelled over her body, and she desperately hoped he would never stop.

But he did.

As though a shot had rung out in the distance, Robert suddenly froze. Lifting his head, he closed his eyes and then stepped back, his hands trembling with the effort it took to release her. "I'm sorry," he whispered, pained eyes looking into hers. "I shouldn't have."

Swallowing, Isabella shook her head. "I asked you to, remember? You have nothing to apologise for."

"Yes, I do." He inhaled deeply. "I betrayed my brother. I kissed his wife. I can't believe I…" Shaking his head, he took another step back, seemingly unable to stand the sight of her.

Feeling the sting of tears in the corners of her eyes, Isabella stepped forward. "Please don't look at me like that."

"Like what?"

"Like you curse the very day you laid eyes on me."

As a heart-breaking sob rose from her throat, he took her hands in his. "I do, and I don't. I can't imagine not knowing you, and yet, if we had never met, neither one of us would be in this horrible situation. We would be better off."

"I know," Isabella said, and the tears spilled forth, running down her cheeks.

Wrapping his arms around her, Robert pulled her against his chest, holding her close and letting her cry.

"Maybe we should tell him," Robert whispered into her hair, and Isabella's head snapped up.

"What?"

Shrugging his shoulders, he looked into her eyes. "I cannot help but think that lying to him is an even greater betrayal than feeling about one another the way we do."

"Do you truly mean that?"

"We cannot help how we feel," Robert said, resignation clouding his eyes. "But we are in control of our actions. We chose not to tell him but to lie to him instead. Even if I leave Bridgemoore, nothing will change, and he won't even know why." Placing a hand under her chin, he made her look at him. "No matter what he does, he won't be able to win your heart, will he?"

Isabella shook her head. "No."

"Then he deserves to know why."

"I already told him," Isabella said, watching his eyes grow wide. "No, I mean I told him that I had lost my heart to another. I didn't tell him it was you. I didn't feel it was my place. But I had to say something. When he came to my bedchamber that night, I couldn't...I just couldn't...I kept wishing he was you."

Robert nodded. "You're right. It was not your place. It is mine." He took a deep breath. "I will tell him."

11

A CONFESSION LONG AWAITED

After changing out of his wet clothes, Robert headed back downstairs toward his brother's study.

When the rain had finally died down a little, he had mounted his mare, pulling Isabella into the saddle in front of him. Wrapping his arms around her to keep the cold wind at bay, he had savoured the feeling of her warm body pressed against his.

Half-way back toward Bridgemoore, they had come across Charles, whose relief upon seeing them safe had only added to the heavy burden resting on Robert's shoulders. He dreaded telling his brother the truth, and yet, he knew his mind would never be at ease if he kept this secret.

Upon their return, Charles had intended to escort Isabella to her bedchamber. However, appearing as though out of nowhere, her mother and sister had instantly gathered around them, clucking like chickens, and had then sent Charles away, themselves tending to Isabella's needs.

An amused smile on his lips, Charles had returned to his own chamber to exchange his soaking wet clothes for dry ones before he went to his study for a drink before supper.

Now, he sat behind his desk, and standing outside the door, Robert could not help but wonder whether or not they would part as enemies that night. Would Charles demand that he leave their family home immediately? If his brother did, would he comply?

Robert shook his head and then rested his forehead against the heavy wooden door. How often had he done so as a boy before knocking and then being called into his father's study to receive yet another punishment?

A wistful smile played on his lips as he finally knocked and then entered.

Rising from his chair, Charles grinned at him. "You look like you could use a drink."

"I wouldn't say no should you offer one." Returning his brother's grin, Robert stepped forward, taking the offered drink with a sigh of relief. It warmed his insides, yet, could not still the trembling in his hands.

"Are you all right?" Charles asked, taking note of his brother's depressed state. "Have you caught a chill? Maybe it would be wise to head to bed early today."

"Maybe," Robert mumbled, setting down his empty glass. Then he lifted his gaze off the floor and met his brother's eyes. "I need to speak to you first though."

"You do?" Charles' eyebrows rose into arches.

Robert nodded and then swallowed, not knowing where to begin. Raking his hands through his hair, he started to pace, occasionally glancing up at his brother. "I know I said I couldn't tell you. I thought it would be better for everyone if you didn't know, but…Maybe I am selfish, but I cannot live like this anymore." He shook his head, trying to clear it. "Look at me! It has only been two days, and I'm a wreck!"

"Then tell me," Charles said. Leaning against the edge of his desk, he crossed his arms over his chest. "Whatever it is, I am glad that you have decided not to keep secrets from me."

Robert nodded, hoping with all his heart that somehow everything would turn out fine. "Before I tell you, I just want to say that I love you. You mean the world to me, Brother, and I never set out to betray you. I never wanted to hurt you. It was the furthest thing from my mind, but…things just happened—I'm not entirely sure how—but..." He took a deep breath. "I just hope that one day, you'll be able to forgive me."

Slightly cocking his head to the side, Charles asked, "It is Isabella, is it not?"

Robert's breath caught in his throat, and he stared at his brother. "But...How do you...?"

The hint of a smile played on Charles' lips as he shook his head and then stepped toward his brother. "You're in love with her, am I right?"

Staring at his brother, Robert felt as though his heart had just stopped beating. "Well, she...I mean, we..."

"Yes or no?" Charles insisted.

Robert drew a deep breath. "Yes."

"Are you certain?" Charles asked. Placing his hands on his brother's shoulders, he looked into Robert's eyes. "Are you certain you love her? Or is this just some infatuation that you won't even remember in a few days?"

Eyes wide, Robert shook his head. "No, I love her. She's..." Still staring at his brother, Robert shook his head. "I don't understand. How do you know? And how can you be so...understanding? Are you not angry with me? I thought you would be furious."

"If I loved her the way you love her, I suppose I would be," Charles said, taking a step back, his eyes still focused on his brother. "She is incredibly important to me, though, and I will not allow her to be used. So, I ask you again: are your intentions honourable?"

"How can you ask me this?" Robert snorted. Had he gone mad? "If I could, I'd marry her in a heartbeat. There, does that answer your question?"

Charles smiled. "It does, yes."

Eyes narrowing, Robert stepped forward, searching his brother's face. "What is going on? Even if you do not love her as much as..."

"As you love her?" Charles finished.

Robert sighed. "Yes. I do not understand why you're not furious with me. She is your wife." He took a step closer, staring at his brother. "Your wife. And I am your brother. How does this not bother you?"

Not blinking, Charles looked at him. "I told you why. Yes, I love Isabella, but not the way you do. Not the way a husband should, I

suppose." He shrugged. "However, we are a good match, or we were until you stole her heart."

"How did you know?" Robert asked. "How long have you known?"

Meeting his brother's eyes, an amused smile curled up Charles's lips. "Dear Brother, simply because you refuse to tell me something does not mean I do not know." Apparently delighted with the shocked expression on Robert's face, he chuckled, "Moments after we had spoken our vows, I knew that something had changed. I could see it plainly on your face and hers. Then later, when I saw you dance with her, the way you looked at her, I thought to myself I had never seen you so bewitched." He laughed. "Don't forget, Brother, I've seen you pursue many a lady before, but none ever held your interest the way Isabella did from the first moment you saw her."

"Why didn't you say anything?" Robert whispered, still dumbfounded by his brother's revelations.

"Well, at first, I wasn't quite certain of either one of your intentions," he admitted. "I didn't want Isabella to get hurt if your interest proved merely temporary or you if I had misinterpreted hers. However, later that night when she confessed to me that someone had stolen her heart, I knew that she spoke of you when she couldn't quite answer my question of why she hadn't told me before the wedding. I told her I would have released her of her promise." A sad smile came to his face as he shook his head. "Of course, she couldn't have. Since you slept in that day, the two of you only met after we were already married."

Robert closed his eyes. Hearing the events of the last two days put in such simple terms, he felt at a loss. Charles was right. If he had only met Isabella before the wedding, things would be different now. But he hadn't, and now she was married to his brother. "I can't believe you knew all this time," Robert whispered. "I was so terrified of hurting you, of losing you. I was sure I would go mad."

"I'm sorry," Charles said, placing a hand on Robert's shoulder. "I suppose I should have said something. I never meant to hurt you either. However, we hadn't seen each other in so long that a part of me couldn't help but wonder if things had changed between us. Despite our differences, we used to be so close, and I really missed that. I just wasn't sure if you did, too. I wanted you to confide in me, Brother, the way you did when we were children. I wanted you to tell me," a deep smile came to his face, "and I'm glad you did."

Pulling him into his arms, Robert hugged his brother as he hadn't since they had been children, and Charles returned his embrace just as warmly. Feeling his eyes grow moist, Robert stepped back and looked into his brother's eyes. "You're right. We should never have drifted apart like this. I should have returned home sooner. I'm sorry."

"You're here now," Charles said, his own eyes glistening as well. "That's all that matters."

Robert nodded, a relieved smile on his face, and yet, he knew that none of this changed the truth. "I'm so sorry," he said, feeling the need to apologise despite his brother's explanations. "I never meant to fall in love with her; with your wife."

"I know that, Robert. I never blamed you. Just like you cannot stop yourself from loving her, I cannot make myself love her. I mean, I love her…just not the way you do; the way she ought to be loved."

Robert frowned. "Then why did you marry her?"

Charles smiled. "Because we suit each other. I can talk to her. We care about the same things, and in many ways, we are very much alike. Neither one of us sought a love match. I suppose we would have been quite happy if you hadn't come along." Charles grinned. "Maybe I shouldn't have invited you to my wedding after all."

Robert laughed, feeling a heavy burden lifted off his shoulders. Despite the mess they still found themselves in, the world was not as bleak as it had been a mere hour ago. With his brother by his side, maybe they could find a way.

Maybe.

Charles sighed. "I don't know what we would have done if I had loved her, too. I suppose then we'd truly have a problem."

"We still do," Robert said, realising that all the hope in the world could not change the fact that his brother was married to the woman he loved. "Even if we both agree that she should be my wife, she is not. She is yours, and there is nothing we can do to change that."

An amused grin came to Charles' face as he looked into Robert's eyes. "You are certainly right that Isabella is married to Charles Dashwood, and that is something we cannot change. However, everything else is open for interpretation."

Shaking his head, Robert stared at his brother. "What on earth are you talking about?"

12

REWARDS & SACRIFICES

nable to believe his ears, Robert looked at his brother. After having accepted that, despite having every reason to be furious with him, Charles was still on his side, Robert still could not understand the delighted gleam that clung to his brother's eyes. "What do you mean?" he asked again. "What is open for interpretation?"

After eyeing his brother carefully, Charles stepped forward, once again placing his hands on Robert's shoulders. "Listen, Big Brother, you are the most important person in the world to me, and I would do anything to see you happy."

Feeling the warmth of his brother's words, Robert smiled at him.

"If you truly love Isabella," Charles continued, his eyes so intently on his brother's that Robert thought he should be able to read his thoughts, "and if you believe in your heart that your love will last, then I will help you."

Robert frowned. "What are you talking about? Nothing can be done. She is your wife. Even if you divorced her, she would still be considered my sister. Even if we would all be willing to live with the social repercussions of such an action, I could never marry her."

"I am not talking about a divorce," Charles said. "You are absolutely right. It is not a solution at all. However, there is another way."

As though his brother had slapped him, Robert's eyes opened wide. Could his brother be serious? Was there truly a way for him and Isabella to be together? How could there be if a divorce was out of the question? If Isabella and his brother didn't get a divorce, they would always be considered married. How could there be another solution?

"However, it would require sacrifices," Charles warned. "Nothing in this world is for free especially in your situation. Do not take this lightly, Robert. You would have to give up who you are in order to be with her. Are you willing to make that sacrifice?"

Robert shook his head, trying to understand what his brother was saying. "Give up who I am? What does that mean? Charles, you speak in riddles. Please just tell me what it is you're suggesting!" Feeling his heart hammering in his chest, Robert took a deep breath. He was starting to feel light-headed.

"Do you remember the summer Father finally agreed to take us to London?" Charles asked.

Robert nodded, the hint of a smile coming to his face. "What was it? Two, three years after *you* shot Mr. Punham?"

Charles chuckled, then sobered and looked at his brother with regretful eyes. "Father was disappointed in you for a long time." He shook his head. "I still cannot believe you did this for me."

Robert shrugged. "It wasn't really such an awful punishment. After all, I never really did want to go to London, at least, not if it meant spending my time in stuffy museums and boring ballrooms."

"Yes, but you were locked inside all summer, and you did feel Father's disappointment. The way he looked at you, did it not make you regret what you had done? Was there never a moment when you wanted to tell him that it had been me?"

Robert shrugged, unsure what his brother was trying to tell him. "Maybe once or twice."

"Then why didn't you?"

"Because it only ever occurred to me when I was mad at you for something," Robert said. "And even then, I knew that should I reveal the truth in a fit of anger, I would regret it later. You're my brother, Charles. There is nothing I wouldn't do for you."

A warm smile spread over his brother's face, and he nodded his head. "I feel the same way."

"I'm glad to hear that," Robert said, "but what does that have to do with the situation we find ourselves in now? Why did you ask me about London?"

"Because during that summer, we heard the story of the Duval Brothers. Do you remember?"

Just when Robert was about to shake his head, a distant memory called to him. "A little," he mumbled, trying to recall details. "Only that they always got into all kinds of trouble."

"They did," Charles nodded. "They enjoyed playing everyone for a fool. Never could they resist the temptation to do so. Not once."

"I remember. But what does that have to do with us?"

Charles chuckled as though Robert was a fool himself for not seeing the answer. "How was it that they always managed to fool people?"

Robert shrugged. "Well, they were twins. They always swapped places, pretending to be the other, especially with people who didn't know they were twins."

"Right," Charles said. "How come we never did that?"

Robert laughed. "Because you just wouldn't, remember? Even as a boy, you were so blasted honourable that you ruined all the fun."

Grinning, Charles nodded. "Well, I suppose the real reason why we would never have been successful lies within our differences. Do you still think that to be true?"

Robert frowned. "That we're different? I suppose so, yes. However, I have to admit that I am beginning to tire of certain aspects of life which I used to think essential to my happiness while at the same time I long for others that I never gave a second thought to before. Does that answer your question?"

"It is a good start."

"A good start?" Robert echoed, starting to feel annoyed. "Charles, please would you just say what you mean?"

"Do you really not know?" his brother asked, eyebrows raised in question. "Have I not given you enough clues?"

"Clues to what? All you did was talk about twins fooling people into believing they were the other." The second the words left his lips, Robert stopped. Raising his eyes to his brother, he found an answering grin on his face. "You're not serious?"

"I am if you are."

Robert shook his head, shocked beyond comprehension. "How can you suggest something like this?"

"It is the only way for you to be happy."

"But...?" Raking his hands through his hair, Robert began to pace the room, occasionally glancing up at his brother, wondering if he had lost his mind.

"If it ensured your happiness, I would not hesitate," Charles stated, his eyes serious again. "However, this is not a decision to be made lightly. We are not talking about playing a prank one afternoon. If we do this, it will be for good. There are many aspects to consider."

Robert stared at his brother. "I can't even think straight." He swallowed. "Just to be clear, you are suggesting that we trade identities...for the rest of our lives?"

Charles nodded, once again stepping up to his brother. "Isabella is married to Charles Dashwood. We cannot change that. The question is do you want to be Charles Dashwood if the prize is her hand in marriage?"

Robert swallowed. "Do I want to be...?" He took a deep breath. "I love her," he said, trying to focus on the one thing that remained a constant in this whirlwind. "I would love nothing more than to be married to her for the rest of my life." He frowned. "But trading identities? Are you serious? Don't you think people will know?"

Charles shrugged. "I am not saying it will be easy. However, we have never fooled people like this as children or even as adults so that it is not something predominant on their minds. However, we will need to adapt our behaviour, both of us." Leaning forward, Charles looked at him intently. "This is not a matter of you cutting your hair and putting on proper clothes."

Looking down at his rather casual attire, Robert chuckled.

"This is about being who we are not," Charles cautioned. "You would need to adapt a more serious and collected demeanour, showing interest in cultural and historical aspects. You would be responsible for Bridgemoore as I have been all those years." Charles paused. "And yet, you would lose your title. Have you thought about that? Your children would not inherit your title."

Robert shrugged. "I never wanted the blasted title to begin with so this aspect is actually good news. But what about you? You would have to be me? Do you think you can do this?"

Charles shrugged, for the first time looking uncertain about the suggestion he had made. "I would do my utmost."

Robert shook his head. "If we are truly going to do this, then we need to make it as easy on ourselves as we possibly can."

"What do you mean?"

He took a deep breath, contemplating what it would be like to trade lives with his brother. "Well, I just think that people will notice if we are to remain in the same lives we have always lived. Maybe we should make a few changes."

"What changes?" Charles asked. "Do you not think that making changes will arouse suspicion?"

"Not necessarily," Robert said. "Listen, when I came back here, I had every intention of leaving again and going back to the life I'd lived before. However, the last few days have truly changed me. Coming home after all this time and seeing you again made me realise that maybe I am ready to settle down myself. Is that so unreasonable?"

Charles shook his head. "I suppose not. So, you are saying, once I am you, I would stay at Bridgemoore and assume the responsibilities of my title?"

Robert nodded. "You have been doing it all along, and I could never do it as well. And after all, it wouldn't be my title anymore, would it?"

"Then what about you?" Charles asked. "It makes me truly sad to suggest this, but maybe it would be a bad idea for us to trade places and then live side by side. In comparison, people are bound to notice."

"I agree," Robert said. "We should think of something." He nodded, and a smile spread over his face. "We will."

Looking at each other, they stood in silence for a moment, each contemplating the future that lay ahead.

"So?" Charles asked. "Are we really going to do this?"

Robert nodded. "If Isabella agrees, then, yes, we are." A smile on his face, he bowed his head. "It is a pleasure meeting you, Lord Norwood."

Shaking his head, Charles grinned. "I am sure the day will come that I will regret this."

Hurrying downstairs, Isabella did her best not to trip over her feet. She breathed a sigh of relief as she stepped off the last stair, glad to find herself on even ground once more. Following the corridor, she soon found herself outside the small back parlour that had seen so many of her tears. How many more would she shed within its walls?

As the door slid open, her eyes were immediately drawn to the pacing man by the back wall. Walking up and down the Persian rug, he occasionally would stop and shake his head or rake his hands through his hair.

Isabella drew in a sharp breath. What would he tell her? She wondered. How had Charles reacted to his brother's confession? Deep down, she had expected her husband to come charging into her chamber, yelling and cursing her name. Only Charles wasn't like that; he wasn't that kind of man. But that didn't mean he couldn't get hurt. Even if he had reacted rationally—as he always did—was his heart now broken? Not because her heart wasn't his, but because his own brother had gone behind his back?

The thought of causing Charles any pain turned Isabella's stomach upside down. As much as she loved Robert, she would never be able to live with herself if their peace of mind was built upon Charles' misery. And yet, speaking the truth had been the only decent course of action, hadn't it?

Stepping inside, Isabella closed the door.

Robert spun around as he heard her approach. A smile spread over his face, and he held out his hands to receive hers.

Feeling her own tremble, she slipped them into his, feeling their warmth engulf her like a warm blanket on a cold winter's night. "What did he say?" she breathed, hearing the blood rush in her ears.

For a moment, Robert just looked at her, seemingly unsure how to respond. Then he shrugged, and a most dazzling smile spread over his face.

Isabella's heart picked up its pace, and yet, she felt more than confused. Why was he smiling? Could he truly be the bearer of good news?

"I don't really know where to begin," Robert finally said. "There is so much to tell you." He took a deep breath. "First, you should know that he is not angry with us."

Isabella closed her eyes as a heavy burden fell from her shoulders. "Thank God," she breathed.

Taking her by the elbow, Robert escorted her to the settee. "Are you all right? Should I call for refreshments?"

Isabella shook her head. "I'm fine." She took a deep breath, and a smile tucked on her lips. "I am just so relieved. He is not angry? Truly? Was he hurt, though?"

Robert shook his head, and Isabella had trouble believing her eyes. "No, he wasn't hurt." He snorted. "He suspected as much."

As the breath caught in her throat, Isabella's eyes went wide. "What? How could he?"

Robert shrugged. "I suppose he is very observant, that brother of mine." Never letting go of her hands, Robert related their talk, and with each word he spoke, Isabella felt like she was experiencing a dream. Could Charles truly be this benevolent? Could he truly wish for them to be together?

Isabella had always known that he didn't love her, at least not the way Robert did. However, he cared for her. To find out that she harboured the feelings she should have had for him for his brother did not cause stirrings of rivalry? Or betrayal?

Smiling, she knew it to be true. Charles was all kindness. She had never seen him angry, always known him to care more for others than for himself. Deep down, she wondered what it would take for him to abandon the calm demeanour he always portrayed and hand over the reins to his own desires.

"I am relieved," she whispered, feeling the sting of tears. "I was so scared that I had destroyed that bond between the two of you. I could never have forgiven m—"

Placing a finger on her lips, Robert stopped her. "Even if..., it wouldn't have been your fault. I did what I did out of my own free will because I could not help myself." He smiled at her. "Because I love you."

As her heart jumped with joy at hearing those very words, Isabella flung herself into Robert's arms. "I love you, too," she whispered, feeling his strong arms close around her, holding her tight. For a moment, she closed her eyes, allowing herself the illusion of what could never be.

If only.

Too soon, Robert sat up, gently removing her arms from around his neck. When he saw her questioning gaze, he smiled. "Do not for a second believe that I do not want you." His eyes twinkled, and as her cheeks grew hot, Isabella averted her eyes. "Listen, there is more that I need to tell you."

Looking up, she wondered what else there was to say. A lump settled in her throat then, and she could barely force out the words. "Are you leaving?"

He squeezed her hands and shook his head. "No. At least, not without you."

"What?" Isabella's eyes went wide as desire fought duty. "We can't. I can't." She shook her head vehemently, trying to convince him as much as herself. "I cannot run away with you."

Again, he smiled at her. "I'm not asking you to."

"Then what are you saying?"

He took a deep breath and swallowed. "As happy as I am that our feelings for each other do not cause Charles the pain I'd feared they would, I know I will never be happy without you by my side."

A sad smile on her face, Isabella squeezed his hand. "Neither will I. But there is nothing we can do. Even if we have Charles' blessing, the law is against us."

"That is true," Robert said, and she wondered at the hope ringing in his voice. What was she missing? "And yet, Charles thought of a way for us to be together."

Isabella's eyes opened wide, and the breath caught in her throat.

Robert held up a hand. "I need to warn you that it is not without sacrifices." He took a deep breath. "However, it is the only way there is."

Isabella nodded, feeling hope swell in her chest, afraid that it would prove to be false. "Tell me," she whispered, nonetheless.

"You are my brother's wife," he said, and her hope fell. "There is no way that you could marry me even if you divorced him."

"Then how...?"

Robert smiled, pulling her closer. "We could be together if Charles and I were to," he took a deep breath, and she could feel a slight tremble run through the hands that held hers, "trade places."

Her eyes opened wide. "What?"

"You are married to Charles Dashwood, and there is nothing we can do about that. But, my brother and I are twins. Who is to say that I am not him? Or that he is not me?"

Staring at him, Isabella couldn't believe her ears. "You cannot be serious?"

Worry began to cloud his eyes. "There is no other way. If you truly love me, then this is all we have. If we don't do this, we will never be together." Seeing the desperate longing in his eyes, Isabella felt her heart soften. "Look, I know that it will not be easy, but would you prefer living the rest of your life without my charming self by your side?" he asked, a twinkle in his eyes as he winked at her. "If you ask me, names matter little. Call me Robert or call me Charles, I do not care. All I care is to have you with me."

Touched by his words, Isabella reached out her hand and placed it on his cheek. He leaned into it then and closed his eyes. "I cannot live without your touch," he whispered and opened his eyes. "Please don't make me. If you truly love me, nothing can stop us."

"Of course, I love you." Taking a deep breath, Isabella looked at him. A million thoughts raced through her head, and yet, all she saw was the future he promised. Was he right? Could they simply trade places and live the life of the other? Would anyone notice? Would she even be married to the man she shared her life with? She had married Charles, and yet, she would be his brother's wife.

Isabella shook her head, feeling overwhelmed. However, when she looked into Robert's eyes, everything suddenly fell away. The only thing left was his love for her and the future within their grasp. "Yes," she whispered as indescribable joy tucked up the corners of her mouth. "Yes."

Robert's face lit up, and before she knew it, she was in his arms. Then he pulled her to her feet, and they danced around the room, laughing and hugging.

"Do you truly believe we can do this?" Isabella asked breathless.

Robert shrugged. "If you ask me, this plan is daring enough for it to work. No one will ever expect it."

"And it was truly Charles' idea?"

Robert laughed. "Believe me; I was as shocked as you are."

"He is a good man."

"The best there ever was," Robert whispered before he drew her into his arms. When her own came up, and her hands caressed his face, he lowered his head and kissed her, enjoying the sweet taste of her and looking forward to many more to come.

13

DUTY & DESIRE

sabella's heart felt like it would burst into a million pieces if she had to wait a minute longer.

Staring at the door to the drawing room, willing it to open, she barely heard what her mother and sister were talking about. Fortunately, they were content even without her contribution. Her father stood somewhere behind her, gazing out the window.

Wringing her hands, Isabella tried to calm her nerves. Would everything go as planned?

"Are you all right, Sister?" Adriana asked, frown lines clouding her face. "You seem tense?"

Her mother's eyes, too, shifted to her clenched hands before a warm hand settled on them, trying to ease the strain. "You have not been yourself lately, *mi corazón*. Tell us what is wrong?"

Isabella tried to smile. "Nothing is wrong. I'm just—"

Fortunately, in that moment, the door finally opened, saving her from having to think of yet another lie to explain her rather strange behaviour these last few days.

"Oh, my goodness!" her mother exclaimed, clasping a hand over her mouth as her eyes widened, taking in the two gentlemen walking into the room.

While Isabella felt herself relax upon seeing them, the rest of her family stared in open-mouthed astonishment at the two young men, who resembled each other in every regard.

In the hopes of their plan succeeding, Robert had regretfully agreed to have his hair cut in exactly the same fashion as his brother. Now, he stood beside Charles, donning the same breeches, the same shirt, the same jacket as his twin. For all intents and purposes, they looked the same.

Watching her family glance from one to the other and seeing the questioning look in their eyes, Isabella smiled, realising that they could not tell them apart.

Relieved, she sighed and then met Robert's eyes.

The second the two men had entered the room, she had known which of them was the man she loved. There was something in his eyes as he looked at her that spoke of his love for her. It was something he could never conceal.

Fortunately, no one else noticed.

"Now, this is an unusual sight," her father laughed. "Are you planning on playing us for fools?" An intrigued smile on his face, he stepped forward, squinting his eyes as they shifted from one to the other. "I cannot tell who is who." He shook his head. "Charles?"

Isabella took a deep breath as Robert stepped forward. "Yes, my lord, it is I." He smiled and then held out his hand to her. Rising from the settee, she hastened to his side, welcoming the warmth of his touch as it chased away the slight chill that had seized her. "I apologise for the confusion," he said, looking at his brother with a somewhat indulgent smile on his face. "However, Robert thought it would be an amusing introduction to his new role here at Bridgemoore."

"New role?" her father echoed, still looking from one twin to the other.

"Yes," Charles said, stepping forward. With a smile on his face, he slightly bowed his head at Robert. "For the past years, Charles has been a most diligent soul, taking care of Bridgemoore and everything connected to the estate and title."

Isabella felt a slight quiver in Robert's hand as he did his utmost to suppress a grin at his brother's words. Glancing at Charles, she thought that he, too, had a tinge of red decorating his cheeks as though embarrassed to sing a hymn of praise about himself.

"Always mindful of his duties—duties that, if truth be told, were never his to begin with—he rarely thought about himself, about what he wanted, about his own dreams." He nodded to Robert and Isabella. "However, now, he finds himself in love with a truly wonderful woman, and I could not be happier for him."

Isabella felt tears gathering in the corners of her eyes. Glancing up at the man she loved, she realised how very lucky she was to be given this chance. If things had been different—if they hadn't been twins, if Charles was not the man he was—she would find herself trapped in a marriage she didn't want, longing for a man she could not have, instead of on the verge of one of the most exciting adventures of her life.

"Therefore, I have decided," Charles continued, "that it is time for me to return to Bridgemoore permanently and finally assume the responsibilities that were mine since the day I was born." With love shining in his eyes, he looked at his brother. "Now, it is your turn, Charles. After all those years of experiencing the world only through the pages of a book, here is your chance to conquer it for real. You have a wonderful woman by your side, and together, you shall see the wonders the world holds for those who dare to look for them."

Holding out his hand, he smiled at Robert, who took it and with an equally touched smile on his face, said, "Thank you, Brother. You have no idea what this means to me."

Charles nodded. "Always have you had my back...since the day we were born. Are you truly surprised that I would do the same for you?"

Robert shook his head. "No, not surprised, just...I cannot find the right words to express my gratitude."

"There is no need," Charles assured him. "I am your brother. Even if you don't tell me, I'll always know."

Shaking his head as though in disbelief, Robert embraced his twin. As they held each other, he closed his eyes, and Isabella knew that he was savouring the moment, knowing it would not repeat itself in the near future.

Stepping back, Charles clasped a hand on Robert's shoulder. "I do not want to see you two back here before the year is out," he said. "Enjoy yourselves. See the world. I will take care of everything; that is my gift to you."

"Thank you, Brother."

Taking a step forward, Isabella placed a hand on Charles' arm. As he turned to look at her, his eyes held the same devotion and love she had seen in them before. Holding her hands in his, he looked deep into her eyes. "Never have I seen Charles as happy as I do now, and the light in your eyes tells me that you, too, have finally found your place in this world."

Touched beyond expression, Isabella nodded, then buried her face in his shoulder and hugged him, unable to find the words to express how grateful she felt.

"You are sending them on a journey?" Adriana asked, and the delighted smile slid from her face. "Where will you go? And for how long?"

Robert shrugged. "I do not know yet."

When Isabella returned to his side, he put his arm around her, holding her close. She looked up at him then and saw in his eyes the memory of the moment that had linked them both forever. Smiling, she turned back to her family, feeling her heart hammer in her chest, and said, "Egypt."

"What?" Adriana gasped.

While the others remained in the drawing room discussing their upcoming journey, Isabella drew her sister aside. They slipped out the terrace doors and headed for the gardens. "Is something wrong?" she asked, feeling the tension in her sister's hand. "You seem not like yourself."

Adrianna shrugged, her eyes fixed on the gravel path below their feet. "It is nothing."

Isabella stopped, pulling her sister back. "Please tell me. I can see that something is bothering you." She swallowed, feeling a strange shiver run down her back. "Is it...Robert?" Saying his name even though it now referred to Charles felt wrong somehow.

Adriana shook her head. Then she met her sister's eyes, and the breath flew from her lungs. "Oh, Isa, I'm so sorry. I do not want to spoil your happiness. Truly! Your smile is so radiant today as I have never before seen it. Obviously you were right. Charles clearly is the right man for you if he puts that twinkle in your eyes."

Isabella chuckled, trying to maintain her composure. A part of her wanted to tell her sister that she had been right all along, that Charles could always only be a good friend. "Then what has you so depressed?"

Adriana sighed. "You will be gone for a long time, won't you?"

Isabella's mouth fell open when she finally realized who had caused the sadness resting in her sister's eyes. How could she have been so blind? "I'm sorry, Adriana. I wasn't thinking. Only a few days ago, I promised you that we would see each other often, and now..."

"Don't be sorry," Adriana objected, brushing a silent tear from her cheek. "I know that, deep down, you've always wanted to see the world, and you deserve to see it," tugging a strand of hair behind Isabella's ear, Adriana smiled, "and at the side of the man who is your perfect match."

"Thank you," Isabella whispered, pulling her sister into her arms. "I will miss you terribly, though."

"You better," Adriana chuckled before stepping back.

Isabella smiled. "What about Robert?"

"What about him?"

"He is dashing, is he not?" Isabella asked, her eyes carefully searching her sister's face, hoping to catch a glimpse of her true feelings.

"I suppose so," was all she said, and Isabella realized that Adriana's interest in Robert had only arisen out of her desire to remain by her sister's side. Touched, Isabella drew her little sister into her arms once more and whispered, "We will be back soon for I could not bear to be separated from you for too long."

"Neither could I," Adriana mumbled. "Neither could I."

EPILOGUE

The candle had almost burned down, and Charles still sat at his late father's desk, staring into the night and wondering what the future would bring.

Before their departure from Bridgemoore, Charles and Robert had spent as much time together as possible, not simply because they enjoyed each other's company, but also because there were many things they did not know about each other's lives. Many days, they had talked long into the night, detailing their whereabouts over the last two years, what acquaintances they had made, the routines they had developed and everything else they could think of.

Naturally, all this information was of less importance to Robert, at least at the moment. However, after their return in one year's time, he, too, would have to find his way through Charles' old life. And although it would seem advisable under the circumstances to keep their lives separate, neither one of them was willing to do so. After reconnecting, it was hard enough to spend one year apart.

Soon, Robert and Isabella would return, and they would all have to find a way to be who they were without arousing suspicion.

Shaking his head, Charles sighed. "I cannot believe I did this," he mumbled, and yet, he knew it never truly had been a choice. How could he not have done it when his brother's happiness had been at stake?

Still, despite being pleased with the outcome of their ingenuity, a sense of dread that he could not explain, much less will away, settled in his stomach. Closing his eyes, he sat back and rubbed his temples, certain that one day someone would discover their ruse.

He could only hope that it would not end in a disaster.

ABOUT BREE

USA Today bestselling author, Bree Wolf has always been a language enthusiast (though not a grammarian!) and is rarely found without a book in her hand or her fingers glued to a keyboard. Trying to find her way, she has taught English as a second language, traveled abroad and worked at a translation agency as well as a law firm in Ireland. She also spent loooong years obtaining a BA in English and Education and an MA in Specialized Translation while wishing she could simply be a writer. Although there is nothing simple about being a writer, her dreams have finally come true.

"A big thanks to my fairy godmother!"

Currently, Bree has found her new home in the historical romance genre, writing Regency novels and novellas. Enjoying the mix of fact and fiction, she occasionally feels like a puppet master (or mistress? Although that sounds weird!), forcing her characters into ever-new situations that will put their strength, their beliefs, their love to the test, hoping that in the end they will triumph and get the happily-ever-after we are all looking for.

If you're an avid reader, sign up for Bree's newsletter at www.breewolf.com as she has the tendency to simply give books away. Find out about freebies, giveaways as well as occasional advance reader copies and read before the book is even on the shelves!

Thanks you very much for reading!

Bree

A Brilliant Rose

(#2 A Forbidden Love Novella Series)

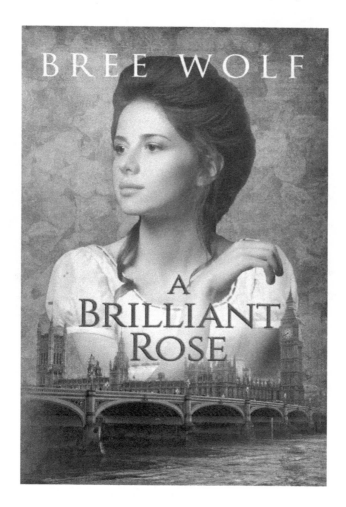

About the book

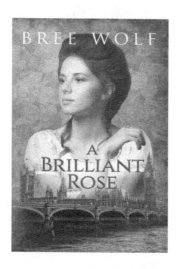

**She is obligated to hate him. Her heart, however, disagrees.
If he cannot prove himself worthy, he will lose her forever.**

When ROSE LAWSON meets a handsome, and yet, intelligent man in the British Museum, she quickly fancies herself in love. However, upon learning the man's name, anger boils within her. She has heard his name before. She knows who he is, and she knows that he is the devil incarnate.

If only her heart and mind didn't disagree so strongly, she could hate him with all the passion she possesses....and he deserves.

Torn from his old life, CHARLES DASHWOOD finds himself wandering the British Museum alone. Gone are his friends with whom he shared his interest in antiquities. Gone is their companionship.

In his desolate state, he comes upon a young lady, who seems to share the very passion he is now forced to ignore. A stimulating conversation ensues, which takes a turn for the worse when she learns his name...or rather his brother's name.

All of a sudden, Charles is faced with a problem not of his own making. From what he can gather, Rose has met him…or rather his brother…before, and unfortunately, her opinion of him could not be lower.

Will Charles be able to win Rose's heart without betraying his brother? Will his brother stand idly by and watch as Charles loses the woman he loves in order to keep his secret?

PROLOGUE

Three Years Ago

Her heart thudding in her chest, Diana tiptoed down the small cobblestone path as her dainty steps echoed through the night air. The moon shone overhead, casting its silvery light into the shadowy dark of the gardens, and from the terrace, the sounds of music and laughter reached her ears. The earl's ball was still in full swing, and to Diana's delight, it had been rather easy to escape her parents' watchful eyes and sneak out into the night.

A part of Diana's mind warned her, cautioned her that such behaviour could have disastrous consequences. Her heart, however, was focused on one thing alone: the man she loved.

If she could only speak to him for a few moments and assure him that his pursuit was indeed most welcome, he would surely speak to her father that very night and ask for her hand in marriage.

At the thought, her breath caught in her throat, and she stopped in her tracks. Drawing the fresh night air into her lungs, Diana sought to steady her nerves. When the slight dizziness that had seized her so unexpectedly finally subsided, she swallowed and then proceeded down the path.

In the dark, the tall-growing hedges and bushes looked ominous, and more than once, Diana drew back with a startled gasp as she feared she had stumbled upon someone lurking in the shadows, intent on doing her harm.

"Where is he?" she mumbled under her breath craning her neck, hoping to catch a glimpse of his tall, striking figure.

After he had asked her to follow him into the night—the gaze in his smouldering eyes saying more than a thousand words ever could—Diana had not hesitated. Ensuring that her parents were otherwise occupied, she had slipped out the terrace doors, following his silhouette until it had disappeared among the shadows.

As the chilled night air brushed over her heated cheeks, Diana's feet carried her onward until, at last, she found the small pavilion as it stood like an island in the midst of a green ocean, its tall, white-washed pillars reaching into the sky.

Sheltered under a canopy roof, his back to her and his strong arms resting on the small rail, he stood motionless on the other side of the small space and stared out into the night.

At the very sight of him, Diana's heart soared, and a rush of emotions swept through her body. Her lips began to tingle at the mere thought of his mouth pressed to hers, and her palms grew moist with nervous anticipation.

Taking another deep breath, she stepped forward, her dainty steps all but silent as she approached him. His intoxicating scent mingled with the soft night smells as the jasmines began to bloom, and Diana thought for a moment she would faint on the spot as her heart raced in her chest.

Coming to stand behind him while desperate to be in his arms, she lifted her hands and softly placed them on the top of his back, gently letting them slide down over his strong muscles.

The moment Diana touched him, he froze...before drawing in a deep breath. "I've been waiting for you," he whispered in that deep, raspy voice that made her breath catch in her throat every time it reached her ears.

A smile spread over her face, and joy filled her heart.

Like a feline, he suddenly spun around and pulled her into his arms, his hungry mouth seeking hers.

Locked in his tight embrace, Diana abandoned all thought as her body responded to his touch as though it recognized him from a previous life. Deep down, Diana had always known that he was her soul mate.

As his lips roamed hers, she held on to him, feeling her knees grow weak. A soft gasp escaped her as his hands travelled upward, and he suddenly drew back.

In the dim light of the moon, he gazed into her eyes, a slight frown curling his brows before he stepped back. "I apologise, Miss—"

"Diana!"

At the sound of her father's enraged voice, Diana's head spun around.

Finding her parents by the tall-growing hedge that shielded the pavilion from passers-by, she swallowed as their disbelieving eyes stared at them, shifting from her to the man by her side.

A smile on her lips, Diana turned to face her parents as they hurried toward them, their own faces pale in the moonlight. "Father, Mother, I can explain."

"I most certainly hope so," her father snapped, his sharp eyes travelling from her to her future husband. "Norwood, what is the meaning of this?"

Clearing his throat, Robert Dashwood stepped forward. "I apologise, sir. There has been some misunderstanding. I—"

"Whatever misunderstanding you thought has occurred, I expect the next words I hear to include a proposal considering the liberties you've just now taken with my daughter!"

With love in her heart and a smile on her face, Diana turned to the man by her side. Butterflies fluttered in her belly as she took a deep breath. *This was it! The moment she had been waiting for her entire life.*

"A proposal?" Laughing, her soul mate shook his head. "I'm afraid I have to disappoint you."

Staring at him, Diana felt the blood rush from her cheeks as the world grew dim around her. "What?" she gasped, her knees suddenly as weak as pudding as the butterflies in her belly died a slow death.

"I apologise," he said, his eyes shifting from her father to her. "As I said, this was a misunderstanding."

"A misunderstanding?" her father boomed as heart-wrenching sobs tore from Diana's throat, and she sank into her mother's arms.

"You take advantage of a young girl and then you refuse to do the only decent thing there is left. What kind of a gentleman are you?"

Chuckling, Lord Norwood leaned against the rail. "The worst kind, I assure you."

"Social etiquette dictates that—"

"I don't care about social etiquette—"

"You will be ruined. Your reputation—"

"My reputation will not suffer, for all of London already knows the kind of man I am." Standing up straight, the notorious viscount stepped forward, fixing her father with serious eyes. "Your daughter, on the other hand, has everything to lose. Therefore, I suggest you be reasonable."

"You downright refuse to marry her?" her father huffed.

"Yes, sir," he confirmed. "You will be well-advised to return to the festivities before we are discovered. No harm has been done so far."

Shaking his head, her father coughed, "No harm? You've compromised her."

"Upon my honour—or what is left of it—it was only a kiss."

Only a kiss? Diana's head spun as she clung to her mother, her hopes crashing into a black abyss that was threatening to swallow her whole. What was happening? Did he not love her? Had he not told her so a million times? Had his loving gaze not spoken the words that his lips had confirmed a mere few minutes ago?

Glaring at the man she loved, her father returned to her side. "You are without honour, Norwood. I sincerely hope that one day you will reap what you sow."

An amused smile on his face, Lord Norwood nodded to her father before his eyes dropped to hers. "All my best to you, Miss...Lawson, is it?" Then he turned and walked away, the shadows swallowing him whole as though he had never been there.

Supported by a parent on either side, Diana placed one step before the other, her mind tormented by the incomprehensibility of what had just happened and her heart aching with the love so unexpectedly ripped from her life.

"I can only hope that Norwood keeps quiet," her father mumbled under his breath, anger still ringing in his sharp voice. "If anyone finds out what happened here tonight, your chances of a favourable match will be ruined."

In that moment, Diana could not bring herself to care. After all, what value could her reputation possibly have when her heart had just been ripped into pieces?

1

IN HIS BROTHER'S SHOES

England 1818 (or a variation thereof)

As the new year began, Bridgemoore found itself covered in a soft layer of snow. The sky gleamed a clear blue dotted with white clouds, and the sun shone brightly, its golden rays reflected in the millions of ice crystals that clung to the frozen ground.

Blinking, Charles Dashwood stepped back from the tall window in his study as the blinding light reached his eyes.

Only the day before, dark clouds had loomed high above the estate like a bad omen for the new year to come. Never would he have expected such a change, and yet, it resonated deep within him.

The old year had ended in a tragedy as Princess Charlotte's death in childbirth as well as the loss of her son had plunged the whole nation into mourning. Black dominated every area of life as people felt the need to express their sorrow. Charles, too, had received the news with a heavy heart.

After losing his own mother early and rather unexpectedly, he was acutely aware of how fragile life could be. Within an instant, the happiness of a moment ago could lie shattered at one's feet. This knowledge had often cautioned him when it came to matters of the heart. Rarely had Charles opened himself up to another human being and the risk of heartache such an action could entail. Only his older twin did he love without restriction.

Months had passed since he had last seen Robert as he and his new bride Isabella had embarked on an adventure that led them around the world. Last he'd heard, they were in Italy.

With a smile on his face, Charles glanced at the tall stack of letters neatly set aside on his desk. Although the two brothers had drifted apart the years prior to the wedding, now they were inseparable as ever—despite the distance that currently lay between them. Rarely a week passed without a new letter from Robert, and Charles could not help but look forward to the day that his brother would return to Bridgemoore.

Once again, his eyes shifted to the powdered world at his feet, stretching to the far horizon, the snow's pure white fading into the sparkling blue of the sky. The world did, indeed, look different that morning—promising—and Charles felt a slight flip in his stomach, hoping that the new year would not fall short of the promises that echoed in his heart that day.

As a knock on the door tore him from his musings, Charles straightened. "Enter," he called and returned to his desk.

With a slightly hesitant step, Mr. Hill walked into the study. "Good morning, my lord."

"Good morning," Charles replied as his steward's unfamiliar address rang in his ears. Although months had passed since he and his brother had switched their identities, which had resulted in Charles' promotion to the rank of a viscount, his mind still stumbled over the undue address, and he could not help but wonder if they had made a mistake.

However, whenever he remembered his brother's glowing eyes as he had looked upon Isabella with love so evident in them, all doubts were dispersed.

Never had he seen two people so much in love, and although Charles cared deeply for Isabella, she was merely a friend to him, a good friend. After all, he had not proposed to her out of love but because they were suited to each other, and she had accepted his proposal for the very same reason. How were they to know that Isabella would find her one true love upon meeting his brother...after she had spoken her marriage vows to Charles?

The only solution to their unfortunate love triangle had been to trade their lives and everything that entailed.

So far, everything had gone smoothly. The past few months at Bridgemoore had passed in mostly the same fashion as before. Despite the fact that Robert as the elder had inherited the title, Charles had always taken care of the estate while his brother had travelled the world, always seeking new adventures. Therefore, Charles simply continued his old routines and dealt with tenants, the upkeep of the estate as well as social responsibilities as he always had.

Only now, he would sign his brother's name; and people would address him as Lord Norwood.

"The repairs to the roof in the east wing are finished, my lord," Mr. Hill, a young man in his mid-twenties, informed him. Although they had been working side by side for the past five years, Mr. Hill now appeared somewhat hesitant and reserved around him, and Charles had to remind himself again and again that the man thought him to be his brother, which would attest to his obvious anxiety. "Now, the wallpaper and furnishings will be replaced as soon as possible." A murderous storm had rolled through the county a few days ago, and a bolt of lightning had almost set the roof aflame. However, the small fire had been quickly extinguished by the torrents of rain pouring from the heavens, only leaving behind a hole in the roof and a soaking wet guest room.

"Thank you," Charles replied, an encouraging smile on his face. "However, there is no rush since the room will not be in use any time soon." He liked Mr. Hill and hoped that the man's unease caused by Robert's rather wild reputation would eventually be soothed through continued respect and civility. "Besides, I will travel to London within a fortnight," he nodded to Mr. Hill, "and will leave the upkeep of Bridgemoore in your capable hands."

A shy smile flitted over the man's face. "Yes, my lord."

"Is that all?"

"Yes, my lord."

"Good," Charles nodded, and once more his eyes shifted to the tall stack of letters. "I would ask you to forward any letters from my brother or his wife that arrive during my absence to my London townhouse immediately."

"I will, my lord," Mr. Hill assured him, his head bobbing up and down. "I will see to everything."

"Thank you," Charles said, noticing with relief that the strain on the young man's face had lessened during their conversation. He could only hope that his absence for the Season would not nourish it once more.

On his way into London, Charles found himself captivated by the dynamic city once again. Ever since his father had taken him into Town over a decade ago to see the Rosetta Stone at the British Museum, he had been taken with the vibrancy that seemed to echo off each and every brick. The streets hummed with the sounds of carts and carriages, hoof beats and voices of animals and people alike, and yet, a serenity hung over the city as though nothing could ever disrupt the rhythm of its existence.

Despite a sense of fatigue that settled on his limbs from the long journey, Charles felt rejuvenated by the city's life force pulsing through his veins. As they drove by Somerset House where the Royal Society was housed, he spotted two old friends from Eton. Delighted, he was about to rap on the roof and ask the coachman to stop when he realised that he was no longer Charles Dashwood.

Sighing, Charles dropped his hand, watching his former friends climb the steps to the front door and vanish inside as his carriage drove by.

By relinquishing his name and identity, he had not only 'gained' his brother's scandalous reputation, but he had also lost his own place in life. No longer was he a member of the Royal Society or the Society of Antiquaries. No longer could he walk up to old friends and discuss the newest developments in all areas of science. No longer could he expect to be taken seriously when voicing his opinion in public.

For years, Charles had observed how people treated or rather thought about his brother. Although few actually disliked him, his reputation for disregarding social etiquette whenever fancy struck him often made him look like a rebellious youth, who simply didn't know any better. On top of that, his boyish charm enchanted and beguiled;

however, it also enforced the ton's general impression that he should not be taken seriously. Were it not for his random love affairs, most people would probably shake their heads at him, an indulgent smile on their faces.

As he climbed the steps to his townhouse, Charles wondered what this Season would bring. Since he was no longer considered a member, he could not possibly spend his time at the Society of Antiquaries, and even though Lord Norwood received an invitation to most events, who would he speak to? More importantly, who would speak to him? And what about?

Shaking his head, Charles sank into the heavy armchair in the back drawing room. Although Robert and he had shared as much of their previous lives with each other before the happy couple had embarked on their journey, Charles felt completely unprepared for the task at hand. How was he to make everyone believe he was his brother? And even if he could, would London be the happy place it had always been for him?

Fortunately, Robert had been abroad the past two years. Therefore, Charles hoped that no recent issues would arise from his brother's past to torment him today.

After a few days of carefully reacquainting himself with the city, Charles found himself in his carriage one night as it slowly made its way to the townhouse of the Earl of Tanwilth. The earl's eldest daughter was to enjoy her first Season this year, and her father obviously intended to provide her with ample opportunity to meet eligible bachelors.

Somewhat startled at the thought, Charles realised that he, too, would be considered an eligible bachelor. Despite his marriage to Isabella, by taking on his brother's identity, he had effectively become a free man once again.

Remembering the way mothers generally eyed Robert with caution and carefully watched their innocent daughters, lest he succeed in seducing them without proposing marriage, Charles wondered if he would ever find a woman that would not only suit him but whose parents would also allow him within speaking distance of her.

Chuckling at the absurdity of the situation he suddenly found himself in, Charles entered the ballroom, his eyes sweeping the many guests in attendance. While he recognised most faces, there were a few he had once counted among his friends.

Of their own accord, his feet moved toward Lord Neswold, an old friend with whom he had shared many an interesting conversation about the three texts inscribed on the Rosetta Stone.

As Charles approached, Neswold turned to him, his eyes narrowed as they slid over his appearance. The good-humoured smile vanished from his face, and he straightened his shoulders. "Norwood."

Taking a deep breath, Charles inclined his head in greeting. "Good evening, it is a splendid night, is it not?"

"It would appear so," Lord Neswold mumbled, clearly wondering why in the world Charles—or rather Robert—was speaking to him. "Have you heard from your brother?" he asked after a moment of uncomfortable silence.

"I have, indeed," Charles said, grateful to have something to say. "He and his wife are currently travelling through Italy."

"That sounds marvellous," Neswold said, and the stern look on his face softened. "Your brother is a good man, and I am glad he is taking this time to enjoy himself."

A self-conscious smile curled up Charles' lips. "He is, thank you."

"I look forward to seeing him upon his return."

Charles nodded and took his leave, sensing that they had reached the end of their conversation.

Fortunately, people seemed to have no doubt that he was, indeed, Viscount Norwood, and, therefore, their secret was not in danger of being revealed. However, Charles could not help but feel a sense of loss, and although he was glad that there was no one at this ball, who had spoken to his brother in the last two years, he wondered how to pass his time that night.

Ultimately, Charles found himself wandering from room to room, exchanging a few pleasantries and greeting people here and there. However, when he tried to speak to old friends of his, the short dialogue that ensued always continued down the same path as the one with Lord Neswold.

Feeling disheartened, Charles returned to the refreshment table, procuring himself a glass of wine. As he stood to the side, watching the happy couples dance the night away to the lively tune played by the orchestra, he wondered about the value of friendship. How differently would this night have gone had he been able to reveal his true self!

"Tonight proves to be a marvellous start into the Season."

Almost choking on his drink, Charles turned in surprise. "Mr. Lawson, it is good to see you!" he beamed, beyond himself with joy that someone would seek his company.

Mr. Lawson, a middle-aged man with laughing eyes, frowned at his reply, and Charles swallowed. "I have to admit I didn't expect you to remember me. After all, it has been years since your father introduced his young boys to me."

"It has," Charles mumbled, searching for an explanation.

Mr. Lawson, however, grinned at him. "Your father always wondered what it would take for you to return to Town."

Charles swallowed, knowing that this was dangerous terrain. Mr. Lawson had been a treasured acquaintance of his father's, and over the years, Charles, too, had shared the occasional conversation with him. After all, Mr. Lawson had spent the previous thirty years working on historical artefacts, such as the Rosetta Stone.

Only too well did Charles remember the spring that he had been introduced to Mr. Lawson. A million questions had flown out of his mouth about the ancient texts chiselled into the stone and their importance for deciphering Egyptian hieroglyphs. Robert, on the other hand, had been bored out of his mind and had voiced his displeasure in his usual frank manner.

Their father had not been pleased.

"I apologise for my inappropriate behaviour back then," Charles said, finding it odd to apologise for something he hadn't done. "I ought not to have spoken as I did."

Laughing, Mr. Lawson waved his apology away. "To be frank, your behaviour was quite within the norm. Few boys that age have an interest in these matters. Your brother was the rare exception."

A delighted smile came to Charles' face. "My...our father always spoke to me...eh...him about the longevity of the world and the small steps its people take on the way to understanding its secrets. It's always fascinated me...I mean, him." Cursing himself, Charles tried to ignore the slightly confused expression on Mr. Lawson's face. "Charles often spoke to me about the marvels of the universe."

Mr. Lawson nodded. "I remember him fondly and was pleased to hear he has found a wife to share these interests. From what I heard, the new Mrs. Dashwood has quite a historical mind herself."

"She does," Charles agreed, mourning the loss of his companion, who had often enriched these nights with her sharp wit. "I believe them to be an excellent match. They are currently travelling the world, for Isabella was quite in raptures about seeing some of the sights she had been reading about with her own eyes."

"I should imagine so," Mr. Lawson said. "I, myself, have always enjoyed travel. It allows us to put the artefacts we discover in a proper context. However, the diligent study of these artefacts is my true passion." He smiled apologetically, and Charles delighted in the childish gleam that came to his eyes. "The secrets they unearth are the very reason I..." He stopped and shook his head as though at himself. "I apologise. I do not mean to bore you with these matters."

Honestly interested, Charles stepped forward. "Not at all. I am eager to hear what you have to say."

Mr. Lawson smiled at him indulgently, and Charles felt reminded of his brother. "Your manners have, indeed, improved," Mr. Lawson chuckled. "If I didn't know any better, I'd believe you to be a dedicated student of the ancient world. However, I do know better, and, therefore, I insist you leave my rather tedious company and join conversations more suited to your interests."

Patting him on the shoulder, Mr. Lawson turned to leave. "It has been a pleasure speaking with you. Next time, I will introduce you to my daughter. Although knowing her as I do, you will probably find her similarly tedious." Laughing, Mr. Lawson returned to the circle of colleagues to which Charles no longer enjoyed the privilege of being acquainted.

Remaining behind, Charles wondered if there was a way for him to openly show interest in the sciences without arousing suspicions. What would people think if he suddenly expressed an interest of joining the Society of Antiquaries?

Sighing, Charles procured himself another drink.

Tomorrow, he would visit the British Museum. That, at the very least, no one could deny him.

LOYALTY

ipping her tea, Rose glanced at her father. Hidden behind *The Times,* he occasionally reached for his muffin or teacup before returning to the words on the page.

Rose cleared her throat, possibly a little too vehemently.

Mr. Lawson, however, as he was completely absorbed in the news of the day, ignored her.

Her lips thinned, and her eyes narrowed. Then she set down her teacup with such force that for a second she feared the saucer had broken.

Lowering the right half of the newspaper, her father glanced at her through squinted eyes. "Would it not be easier to voice your objections verbally, my dear?" The hint of a grin tickled his lips. "If you continue to destroy our good china in order to get my attention, what will we drink from in the future?"

Rolling her eyes, Rose shook her head. "As always you're exaggerating, Father. It was one teacup."

"And one saucer if I recall correctly." Setting down the paper, her father turned to her, a twinkle in his eyes and a mischievous grin on his face.

Some days, Rose swore he was a young boy trapped in an old man's body!

A scientist at heart, her father had married late in life as no woman could compete with his one true love. Only after her mother had died in childbirth had Mr. Lawson realised that there was an even greater miracle in his life than the study of ancient societies. From the moment the midwife had laid Rose in his arms, he had doted on her as any devoted father would.

As far as Rose could remember, they had never spent a day apart. Unlike other fathers, he had never felt the need to appear too respectable. Crawling around in her nursery on all fours with her on his back, they had spent many a wonderful day. He had taught her to read and write and opened up his world to her without hesitation, delighted with her hungry mind and quick wit. Many days, Rose had accompanied him in his work, learning Latin and Greek, hoping to understand the few remnants left by societies past. Their conversations had always been a source of joy for her because only in her father's company did Rose feel truly accepted for who she was.

"What can I do for you, my dear?" he asked, his eyes earnest as they searched her face. "You seem distraught."

"I am." Taking a deep breath, Rose met her father's gaze. "I am worried about Diana."

Rolling his eyes, her father huffed something unintelligible before picking up his newspaper once again.

Frowning, Rose stared at him. "How can you not care about her misery? She is your niece, after all."

"What misery?" Dropping the paper, her father shook his head as red blotches crawled up his face. He took a deep breath, trying to remain calm. "I love her dearly, but that girl is a spoiled chit!"

Rose's mouth fell open.

"I mean no disrespect," her father continued before she could object, "but as an only child, she has always gotten whatever she wanted, and she expects no less of the world."

"I am an only child as well," Rose pointed out. "Do I dare ask what you think of me?"

For a moment, her father stared at her, then the agitation left his face, and he reached out, gently placing his hand on hers. "My dear Rose, maybe you are right not to blame her for her faults because, after all, it was her parents who indulged her every whim and turned her into the woman she is today."

Rose knew his words to be true. As the firstborn son, her uncle had inherited the title of a baron as well as the family estate and its financial resources. When after a number of miscarriages, Diana had been born, both, he and his wife, had been overjoyed, spoiling her to no ends. As a result, Diana had turned into a spoiled chit—as her father had called her—demanding that everything was carried out precisely as she desired.

However, Rose also knew—while her father did not—the very reason why Diana's life had suddenly become such a burden to her.

Meeting her father's caring eyes, Rose knew that she could never reveal to him her cousin's secret as Diana had sworn her to secrecy.

Her father nodded, and the hint of a smile lit up his face. "However, I am guilty of the same transgression, and yet, you have become a woman who makes me proud every day."

Not only his words, but also the love that shone in his eyes brought tears to her own, and a deep smile came to her face. "Thank you, Father."

"Don't thank me," he said, patting her hand. "I suppose it is not because of my influence, but rather in spite of it, that you turned into such a marvellous, young woman," he chuckled. "However, I fear that London society will never know considering that you missed your first ball last night. I thought you were at least somewhat excited about your first Season in Town."

"I am," Rose assured him. "However, Diana needed me, and I could not leave her."

Rolling his eyes once again, her father shook his head. "Did she not just have a baby?" he asked. "I thought women enjoyed motherhood. What could she possibly be complaining about now?"

"Women are not solely on this earth to be mothers," Rose snapped, wondering where that hint of anger had come from.

Not offended in the least, her father grinned, patting her hand once again. "I apologise if I have offended your sensitivities, my dear. I know very well—"

"I wish you wouldn't treat me like a delicate flower," Rose interrupted. "Say what you have to say, and do not apologise for it."

"As you wish, my dear Rose." A mischievous gleam came to his eyes as he chuckled into his beard. "What I meant to say—before you so rudely interrupted me—was that I know very well how capable women are. After all, I have you to remind me of that every day."

"Thank you," Rose mumbled, a slight blush colouring her cheeks as she regretted her rather inappropriate outburst.

"If I am not to apologise, then you are not to thank me." Her father held out his hand to her. "Do we have an agreement?"

A smile on her face, she took his hand.

"Promise me you will do something entertaining today," her father said. "Spending your days listening to your cousin's imagined complaints cannot be good for your health." He glanced at the paper, then met her eyes again. "How about a visit to the British Museum? That place always brings the most wonderful glow to your eyes."

Rose nodded. "That is a splendid idea, Father."

"I wish you wouldn't sound so surprised!"

Chuckling, Rose reached for her teacup. "I will go and ask Diana if she wants to accompany me."

Dropping the paper, her father stared at her. "That is not what I had in mind. Do you misunderstand me on purpose?"

"No, not at all. However, you are right. Diana needs to get out for a little while and do something enjoyable. Maybe it will lift her spirits."

Folding the paper, her father leaned forward, resting his forearms on the table. "First, I was talking about you, not Diana. Second, as far as I know, that girl cares very little for artefacts of any kind."

Rose shrugged. "Maybe I can change her mind."

Shaking his head, her father chuckled. "Learn to recognise a lost battle, my dear. It will save you heartbreak and disappointment." Before Rose could object, he lifted a hand to stop her. "Since I know my niece—and I know she'll have no interest in cultivating her knowledge on ancient societies—I shall stop by her townhouse around noon and escort you to the museum myself, thereby ensuring that you will not spend the whole day catering to Diana's every need." Her father's eyes narrowed as he regarded her. "Or do you have any objections?"

Rose shook her head. "I do not, Father. Thank you, for I truly wish to see the stone again."

Although only two years Rose's senior, Diana deported herself like an old woman whenever her *imagined complaints*—as Rose's father called them—plagued her. Whining and wailing, she moved from the settee to the armchair and back again, a moist handkerchief draped over her forehead so as to soothe the migraine that had assailed her once again. Whenever her spirits were low, she was a nightmare to be around, and yet, Rose could not help but pity her for the losses she had suffered.

"Maybe you should return to your bedchamber," Rose suggested, suspiciously eyeing the brilliant sunlight reaching inside the drawing room through the wide-open curtains. "The dark will ease the pain and allow you to rest."

"Rest?" Diana shrieked, her head jerking off the backrest of the armchair. "I would rather die than spend another day locked up in that room, all alone in the dark."

Rose sighed. Her cousin's fits of melodramatic exaggeration exhausted her. "You were not locked up, Diana. You were in childbed," she reminded her, hoping that the thought of her new-born son would bring a smile to her face.

It did not.

"Dear Cousin, if you knew what childbirth meant," Diana spat, "you would not speak of it as though it were a delight." Sinking back into the armchair, she closed her eyes.

"You are right," Rose conceded. "I do not know. However, your son is born now. Do you not delight in his presence?" Remembering the sweet, little boy, a wistful smile came to Rose's lips. "Is he not a blessing?"

"A blessing?" her cousin echoed, incomprehension ringing in her voice as she met Rose's gaze. "How could he be? He only reminds me of the man I was forced to marry."

Sitting down across from her cousin, Rose looked deep into Diana's eyes, hoping that her cousin would listen to the words she needed to hear. "I feel for you, Diana. I truly do," Rose said, and relief washed over her when her cousin's features softened. "I know how ill you were treated and how that forced you down a road you would not have chosen for yourself. However," reaching out, she grasped her cousin's hand, "what is done is done. You cannot change the past. Are you willing to sacrifice your future for a man who only treated you with disregard?"

Tears streamed down Diana's face. "It was just one night. One foolish night, and now I live with regret every day."

"I know."

"I should never have trusted him," Diana whispered, wiping the moist handkerchief over her flushed face. "I know the words you speak are true, dear Cousin. However, it is easier said than done."

"Why?" Rose asked, afraid that the moment of honest reflection would slip from her grasp. How many times had she pleaded with Diana to leave the past behind? Countless times. Wallowing in her pain, her cousin had never listened, never understood a word Rose had said. "It is only your own pain and regret that keep you from moving forward."

Diana took a deep breath, then she closed her eyes and shook her head. "It is not." Meeting Rose's gaze, she sat up. "I hear he has returned to Town." Rose swallowed. "How am I to walk with my head held high when the whispers will start anew now that he is back?"

"I didn't know," Rose admitted, suddenly feeling defeated. "When did he arrive back in Town?"

"From what I heard he returned to England for his brother's wedding and has spent the last few months at his family's estate." She met Rose's eyes then, deep pain only too visible in them. "He has been in London these two weeks past."

Rose looked at her cousin through narrowed eyes, and what she saw whipped the air from her lungs. Despite everything that had happened, Diana still cared for the man who had broken her heart. If he were to call on her, she would not be able to send him away.

Rose shivered at the thought.

A baby's cries echoed through the halls, and Diana squeezed her eyes shut. "He has been doing this all night!"

"He needs you," Rose reminded her, feeling her own heart go out to the helpless infant. Why was it that Diana was immune to the needs of her own son? "You are his mother. Go to him."

"I have a nursemaid for that," Diana objected, shaking her head determinedly.

"You need him, too," Rose insisted. "He is the only one who can heal your heart."

Diana snorted. "Puh! He is his father's son. And such an awful name...Benedict." She shook herself as though ill. "That silly family tradition of giving the first born son his father's middle name. Ugh! He will never find a wife with that name. Just like his father, there is nothing appealing about him. Despite his fortune, no woman in her right mind would ever have agreed to marry him." Closing her eyes, Diana sighed. "Neither would I. Only I didn't have a choice."

"Come outside with me," Rose urged her. "It is not good for you to spend all your time indoors, regretting what was." A tentative smile came to Diana's face. "I promised my father to go to the British Museum today; come with me!"

Diana slumped back in her chair. "Go without me. The last thing I need right now is a stuffy museum. In all honesty, I cannot understand what makes you enjoy it so." Closing her eyes, she draped the handkerchief back over her eyes while her son's cries echoed from the second floor.

3

A KINDRED SOUL

*A*scending the first two stairs to Montagu House, Rose lifted her head and gazed up at the stately manor that housed the British Museum. Under its roof, large collections of artefacts had found their final resting place, and whenever Rose set foot over its threshold, a chill went down her back as though these artefacts were not soulless objects but filled with the spirits of times past, eager to share their secrets with her.

"Ah! There it is," her father exclaimed, and Rose turned her head to look at him.

"There is what?"

"The glowing smile that rivals the sun," he said, his eyes sweeping over her in unadulterated happiness. "I shall be back shortly. Enjoy yourself! However, I have no doubt that you will."

"Thank you, Father, for not saying *I told you so.*"

Suppressing a grin, he nodded. "I would never dream of it."

After being admitted, she ventured through the lower floor, awed by the large library, its rows upon rows of books filling the walls on all sides of her. If she only had the time to read them all! She mused, *What would it feel like to possess the knowledge gathered in these volumes? What wisdom would they bring?*

Heading upstairs, Rose ran her eyes over the various modern works of art located on the upper floor, and while she appreciated their unique essence, her feet were irrevocably drawn to the gallery.

Not once did her gaze travel to the other visitors, who were engrossed in the artefacts on display just as much as her. Their hushed voices and quiet footsteps mingled into a soft melody that soothed her rattled mind and comforted her aching heart.

Approaching the gallery, everything fell away, and for one pure moment, Rose felt liberated of the burdens that plagued her.

Feasting her eyes on the sight before her, Rose sighed. The gallery was by far her most favourite place in the world!

Beautifully crafted terra cottas, drawings and engravings lined the walls, and Greek and Roman sculptures decorated the room, hinting at societies long gone while Sir William Hamilton's collection of Greek vases allowed for a rare view of ancient life.

"Beautiful," Rose whispered as her mind absorbed the small details of various illustrations, guessing at their importance, at their meaning for the world today.

Lost in her own musings, Rose suddenly found herself standing in the one spot that held her heart. Without conscious thought, her feet would always direct her here as though it called to her. Lifting her head, she gazed almost lovingly at the Rosetta Stone.

A large, black granite rock, it held a decree issued in the times of the Pharaohs in Ancient Egypt. What was unusual was that the decree was written in three scripts: Ancient Egyptian hieroglyphs, Demotic script and Ancient Greek. However, so far no one had been able to decipher every last one of the words written there; the Ancient Egyptian hieroglyphs posed a problem.

Marvelling at the fine line between knowing and not knowing, Rose smiled, whispering her father's favourite Greek quote, "Εν οίδα ότι ουδέν οίδα." It seemed appropriate considering the vastness of yet undiscovered knowledge.

"I know one thing that I know nothing," a deep and rather surprised sounding voice spoke out behind her, and Rose spun around, startled.

Wide-eyed, she jerked up her head and stared at the tall man standing before her as his eyes shifted from the stone to meet hers, a delighted twinkle in them. Strong with broad shoulders, he towered above her. His gentle features, though, spoke of a kind and honest man, and Rose exhaled the breath she had been holding.

His gaze held hers, and an enchanting smile curled up his lips. "I have never before met a woman who could quote Socrates and in Ancient Greek, too."

As the honest admiration in his words resonated within her, Rose found herself swept away by his deep hazel eyes which looked into hers as though she herself were a rare artefact.

Feeling suddenly flustered, Rose averted her gaze; after all, it was not proper to stare at a stranger. "It is my father's favourite saying," she explained, grateful to have something to say. "He feels the lack of knowledge is its own greatest asset as it motivates us to understand what we do not know."

His brows rose into arches as he nodded his head. "I suppose few people would consider lack of knowledge a desirable state. However, I do see the wisdom in your father's words. He, himself, must be a man of great knowledge to have come to that conclusion."

Rose chuckled, "I do believe so. However, my father would not agree with your judgement of him."

Instead of surprise, understanding curled up the corners of his mouth. "He would not? Would you say it is modesty which keeps him from admitting to the wisdom he possesses? Or rather the desire to lower the expectations of others?"

Feeling herself smile up at him openly, Rose cleared her throat. "While my father claims that he does not know nearly enough to be called wise, in my opinion, he is merely afraid to disappoint, yes." Delighted with their conversation, Rose searched her mind for something else to say. Never before had a man besides her father spoken to her as though her mind was equal to his.

As she looked at this stranger, who had appeared out of nowhere, she saw no hint of superiority or condescension in his eyes. Instead, she saw the same desire to understand, to gain knowledge and to see the world for all its possibilities.

Where had this man been all her life?

As his feet carried him up the stairs and toward the gallery, Charles felt as though he were coming home. Although the museum had acquired new artefacts since the last time he had visited, the Rosetta Stone called to him.

When his father had taken him to London that first summer, the visit to the British Museum had marked Charles's first steps into the historical societies that had been his home these past ten years. Back then, it had been this ancient stone, newly arrived from Egypt, that had drawn visitors from far and near, and to this day, to Charles, it was the embodiment of the possibilities of ancient knowledge.

However, as he approached the stone, he found his usual spot occupied by a young woman of medium height. Her golden-red hair rested softly on her slender shoulders as her eyes swept almost lovingly over the finely chiselled inscriptions. Something about the way she held her head slightly bowed, her hands linked as though in prayer, spoke to him, and he drew near.

Debating what to do, he stood behind her right shoulder for a short while as his eyes went back and forth between her and the stone.

Then a soft smile touched her lips, and she drew a deep breath before whispering, "Εν οίδα ότι ουδέν οίδα."

Like a punch to the gut, her words knocked the air from his lungs. It was as though she had whispered a secret password, one that identified her as a kindred soul, and Charles knew that he could not stand back and allow her to disappear from his life. He knew he ought not to address her. However, the need to reveal himself to her was stronger than anything he had ever experienced, so he opened his mouth and answered her unintentional call, "I know one thing that I know nothing."

Instantly, her shoulders tensed, and she spun around, round emerald eyes staring up into his.

Cursing himself, Charles smiled at her reassuringly, hoping that he had not just destroyed any chance of gaining her favour. "I have never before met a woman who could quote Socrates—and in Ancient Greek, too," he said, trying to express the emotions that raged through his heart.

Here, before him, was a like-minded soul, and he desperately wished to speak to her, hear her opinions and learn her thoughts with regard to the many questions that remained still unanswered despite the many secrets already uncovered.

And while his mind marvelled at the wonderful coincidence that had brought them both here this day, his heart whispered that the soft glow in her dark green eyes was unlike any other he had ever seen.

A gentle flush rose to her cheeks, and for a moment, she bowed her head. "It is my father's favourite saying," she replied, meeting his eyes once again, and he saw in her own the same surprise he felt in his heart. "He feels the lack of knowledge is its own greatest asset as it motivates us to understand what we do not know."

Delighted with the depth of their conversation, Charles nodded his head. "I suppose few people would consider lack of knowledge a desirable state." Meeting her eyes, he smiled. "However, I do see the wisdom in your father's words. He, himself, must be a man of great knowledge to have come to that conclusion."

A soft chuckle escaped her rosy lips, and the sound echoed through his heart with such tenderness that Charles had to draw a deep breath to steady himself. "I do believe so," she replied, deep affection ringing in her voice. "However, my father would not agree with your judgement of him."

Remembering his own father's thoughts that everything learnt could always be surpassed, that around the next corner waited another mind ready to challenge what he thought he knew to be true and possible, Charles nodded. "He would not? Would you say it is modesty which keeps him from admitting to the wisdom he possesses? Or rather the desire to lower the expectations of others?"

Another soft smile curled up the corners of her mouth. "While my father claims that he does not know nearly enough to be called wise, in my opinion, he is merely afraid to disappoint, yes."

Returning her smile, Charles said, "I suppose only truly wise men will ever refute any such claim. They know that wisdom is nothing to be truly gained and thus possessed for it is a futile state, always subject to change."

A gentle frown came to her face, and for a moment she seemed unsure whether or not to express what was on her mind. When she finally spoke, Charles' heart skipped a beat. "Would you restrict such a statement to men alone?"

Seeing the serious expression in her eyes, Charles understood the struggles she had faced in being recognised for the beautiful and frankly capable mind she possessed. "Not at all," he assured her. "Forgive me for my poor choice of words. Wisdom and knowledge do not differentiate between men and women; they see them as equals."

A radiant smile came to her face, and Charles suddenly felt the desire to cup his hand to her soft cheek. "Would you consider knowledge to be the same as wisdom?" she enquired next, and Charles felt as though he was being weighed.

"Not at all," he assured her once more, glad to see relief flash over her face. "Many people possess knowledge without the wisdom to understand and use it properly. Wisdom, however, exists away from knowledge and is far more difficult to acquire than knowledge."

"I do agree," she said, and her eyes shone with pure, unadulterated joy, the same joy that pulsed through his own veins. "I suppose wisdom is gained through deep reflection and careful consideration and by learning from others." Her eyes shifted to the Rosetta Stone, and a rueful smile curled up her lips.

"I assume you come here frequently," Charles observed, and she turned back to look at him, "for you seem quite familiar with this artefact."

She nodded eagerly. "I am. My father spent years of his life studying it, believing it to be the key to understanding Egyptian hieroglyphs. When he first heard of its discovery, he wept with joy for it was the day I was born, and he believed it to be a sign from the heavens." She smiled up at him, and her eyes met his openly. "I am named for this stone."

"Rose," Charles whispered, staring at her in awe before she nodded her head, a shy smile illuminating her beautiful face. Clearing his throat, Charles said, "It is a beautiful name, indeed."

Suddenly remembering his manners, he stepped forward and inclined his head to her. "I apologise. I should have introduced myself earlier." Deep down, he knew that he should never have spoken to her; however, he could not bring himself to regret his actions. "Robert Dashwood, at your service." Relieved to hear himself give his brother's name, Charles smiled at her.

The eyes that looked into his suddenly changed. The soft twinkle that he had seen there only a moment ago disappeared as her mouth opened, and she mumbled, "Robert Dashwood. You are...?"

Swallowing, she stepped back, her features hardening as she glared at him with what could only be described as hatred and disgust mixed into an emotion so deep and so absolute that it froze the blood in his veins.

The smile slid off his face then, and he stared back at her, desperately hoping that it had all been a mirage, that somehow his eyes had deceived him.

However, they had not.

"Is something wrong?" Charles asked as he helplessly watched the connection between them dissolve as though it had never existed; worse even for instead of indifference, he found himself fixed with a hateful glare, an abyss impossible to bridge.

All colour left her face, and the beautiful curl of her full lips thinned into a tight line. "I need to leave," she snapped, rushing past him.

Spinning around, Charles stared after her as she hastened toward the large staircase. His soul screamed at him to stop her; however, deep down, he knew that there was nothing in his power that could persuade her to stay.

As her footsteps echoed through the high-ceilinged room, Charles felt his spirits sink even lower than the day he had realised how isolated he suddenly was, even in a large city as London. Meeting her here today by chance, had been the ray of sunshine fighting its way through a dark overcast sky, touching the earth in but a single spot, allowing the dying flower to bloom again.

Sighing, Charles closed his eyes. What had changed? Why had she run from him? His name. He realised. She had only run from him after he had given her his name. No, not his name, but his brother's name. Had she known Robert? What reason could she possibly have to despise him the way she clearly did?

Well-aware of his brother's scandalous reputation, Charles groaned. Although he had never asked Robert for details, Charles had always allowed himself to believe that his brother would never take advantage of a young girl as sweet and innocent as Rose.

But what if he had been wrong?

A FORBIDDEN LOVE
NOVELLA SERIES

More to follow!

www.breewolf.com

LOVE'S SECOND CHANCE SERIES

For more information, visit

www.breewolf.com